A PLAGUE ON BOTH YOUR HOUSES

BOOKS BY ROBERT LITTELL

NOVELS

The Defection of A. J. Lewinter

Sweet Reason

The October Circle

Mother Russia

The Debriefing

The Amateur

The Sisters

The Once and Future Spy

An Agent in Place

The Visiting Professor

Walking Back the Cat

The Revolutionist

The Company

Legends

Vicious Circle

The Stalin Epigram

Young Philby

A Nasty Piece of Work

The Mayakovsky Tapes

Comrade Koba

A Plague on Both Your Houses

NONFICTION

For the Future of Israel (with Shimon Peres)

A NOVEL IN THE SHADOW OF THE RUSSIAN MAFIA

A PLAGUE ON BOTH YOUR HOUSES

ROBERT LITTELL

BLACKSTONE PUBLISHING

Published in 2024 by Blackstone Publishing
Cover design by Bookfly Design

Printed in the United States of America
Originally published in hardcover by Blackstone Publishing in 2024

First paperback edition: 2024
ISBN 979-8-212-63835-7
Fiction / Thrillers / Historical

Version 1

Blackstone Publishing
31 Mistletoe Rd.
Ashland, OR 97520

www.BlackstonePublishing.com

Again and always, for Victoria

Absent a sister revolution—somewhere, anywhere, fuck, everywhere!*—your bloody Bolsheviks have a lot in common with lemmings asking directions to the nearest cliff.*

—The British bird Ophelia,
nostalgic for Leon Trotsky
and Willy Shake Shaft

A plague o' both your houses! They have made worms' meat of me.

—Mercutio's dying words
in Shakespeare's *Romeo and Juliet*

1
TIMUR THE LAME: THE STOOL PIGEON SWALLOWED HIS PILLOW . . .

STRICT REGIME CORRECTIVE LABOR COLONY NO. 40,
KUNGUR, PERM REGION
Saturday, December 25, 1971

When the Ossete boy was born with one leg half a hand shorter than the other he was given the name Timur, after Shuja-ud-din Timur, the brutal Mongol conqueror of Persia known to the world by his Tartar name, Tamerlane—Timur the Lame. At fourteen Timur fled the backwater Georgian village of Areshperani and made his way to Moscow, where, days after he landed in the capital, he was arrested while picking pockets in a metro station when he couldn't outrun two plainclothes detectives. Worried that the lady judge would consider him too young and too lame to send to prison, the Chekists broke three fingers of his right hand and his nose. The fingers eventually healed; the aquiline nose, badly set in a neighborhood clinic, didn't; one nostril produced a slight whistle when he talked excitedly.

Forty years later Timur is the *pakhan*—the godfather, or *capo dei capi*—of the thirty-eight Ossete *vory v zakone*, literally *thieves-in-law.* Professional thieves who pride themselves on living by a strict code of honor, they are billeted in the windowless attic of a barrack, one of two dozen wind-sanded wooden buildings planted in neat rows on an ice-crusted steppe so bleak no wall is needed to keep prisoners from escaping. The rings tattooed onto the middle fingers of his left hand—three tiny onion-shaped domes draped in barbed wire—signify his status as a *vory vozhd*, or guide. He is, as the senior *vor* in Labor Colony No. 40, the shadow camp commandant who maintains order—or provokes disorder when it suits him. Nothing happens in the *zona*—not the murder of a *vor* by other *vory*, not the stabbing of a Muslim guard by Orthodox guards, not the gang rape of a new female prisoner by other *zeks*, male or female—without the consent of the *pakhan*.

It is minus twenty-eight degrees Celsius outside, minus four inside thanks to the wood-burning stove in the attic; Timur's Ossete *zeks* have piles of broken wooden chairs, broken wooden bunk beds, and broken benches, along with a heap of split birch logs, that they feed into the potbelly stove. The Ossetes, who are forbidden by their *vory* code to do prison work, spend their waking hours playing backgammon or doing push-ups or daydreaming of life before prison—or, if they manage to survive the strict regime of Corrective Labor Colony No. 40, life *after* prison. The *zeks* who have had some schooling read; the ones who can't read are read to. Like the camp guards, the Ossetes sleep on double-deck bunks fitted with thick army mattresses and pillows (unlike the common *zeks* below, who sleep on wooden planks covered with straw, or the floor). The *pakhan* wears a woolen turtleneck sweater under a washed-out blue jumpsuit with his prisoner ID Ф7532319Ж stenciled over the breast pocket, a quilted knee-length coat, leather galoshes (one of which is fitted with an unusually thick sole and heel) two sizes too large so he can stuff them with rags to prevent frostbite, and a knitted sailor's cap pulled over his ears. Like all his Ossete *vory*, he has a telltale tattoo on his right breast: a small but perfect portrait of Vladimir Lenin. The tattoo conceals a coded message: *Vladimir Organizer of Revolution*, or *VOR*—the Russian word for *thief*. Not *thief-in-law*, like Timur and his Ossetes, but just plain *thief*. The *vory v zakone* loathe Vladimir Lenin, Iosif Stalin (even though the late unlamented despot was said to have had Ossete blood from his father's father in his veins), and Communists in general. The bastards didn't change Russia, Timur has been heard to say, a few still have more than they need, most still need more than they have. The *vory* also disesteem Jews—"strange animals reeking of the ghetto, jabbering a weird Yiddish"—in the belief that an international Jewish conspiracy was behind the Bolshevik Revolution that brought Lenin and Stalin and the Communists to power.

Two guards can be heard climbing the ladder to the attic. The one carrying a wooden crate filled with liter bottles of Soviet beer shoulders open the trapdoor, then holds it up for the second guard carrying a big soot-black stockpot of steaming goulash. Setting it down, he retrieves the carton of Bulgarian cigarettes from the deep leg pocket of his paratrooper khakis, along with the packet of mint chocolates for Timur. The thing the *pakhan* misses most in the *zona* isn't cigarettes or vodka but chocolates. They remind him of his lost youth back in Areshperani on the Caspian steppe, when his mother would reward him with a single chocolate if he brought home a good note on his end-of-month report.

Stashing the chocolates in the kit under his bunk, the *pakhan* nods to Cephalus Papachristodoulopoulos, known as "the Greek" because the Ossetes have trouble remembering his name and the very few who remember it have difficulty pronouncing it.

The offspring of an Ossete wet nurse and a Greek mineralogist trapped in Georgia during the Great Patriotic War, the Greek is the keeper of the *vory obshchak*, the thieves' common fund. Like all of Timur's *vory*, he has rings tattooed on the fingers of his left hand. The rings represent a kind of passport to the thieves' world, recounting how many times he's been sentenced to prison (twice), how many years he has served (twelve), and for what crimes (extortion and illegal foreign exchange dealings under Article 88 of the Soviet Criminal Code). The Greek retrieves an iron box from under his bunk, opens the combination lock, and counts out rubles to pay off the guards.

Moistening his thumb with his tongue, the guard in the paratrooper khakis double-checks the sum. "You are ten rubles shy, Greek," he complains. "Chocolate is more expensive than gold in this Perm wasteland. The packet costs eighty rubles now."

"It was seventy last month," the Greek remembers.

The guard shrugs. "We are all of us prisoners of inflation."

Slipping a ten-ruble bill onto the pile in the guard's palm, the Greek glances at Timur. "You eat too much chocolate, *pakhan*," he calls over to him with a barely suppressed laugh. "Your sweet tooth will be the death of you one day."

"Good a way to croak as any," Timur snaps back.

Spare Rib starts to ladle goulash onto mess tins set out on the long wooden table.

"Bring the poet up," Timur instructs the Greek.

The poet, gaunt, unshaven, with a filthy blanket draped over his shoulder like a shawl, slowly climbs the ladder to the attic. One sole of his city shoes flaps loose as he walks. Timur nods for the poet to take a seat on the bench around the table, and a plate of steaming goulash is set in front of him. He eats with a metal spoon, chewing delicately because of his bleeding gums. Timur and the other *zeks* slide onto the benches around the table, pry off the metal caps on the beers, press their thumbs over the necks of the bottles, and shake them to get some bubbles into the flat Soviet brew. The poet, his eyes bloodshot with fear, pushes away his plate, pulls a tattered book from his pocket, and begins to read in an almost inaudible voice that the *zeks* must strain to hear.

Timur, his elbows on the table, his head propped in the palm of one hand, eyes the poet. "Louder, if you please," he gently instructs him.

> I'm sitting behind bars in the dank, dark cell,
> As a captive eagle, born and bred in the jail,
> My crestfallen cage mate, with his wings
> widespread,
> Pecks at scraps of food I set on the ledge.
>
> He's pecking and looking at me through
> the bars,
> And sharing a thought as common as stars.
> He summons me with a glance and a cry,
> As if to say, "Come, let us fly!"
>
> We prisoners are free as birds; it is time,
> birds of a feather,
> To fly to haze-covered peaks together,
> To fly where the blue of the sea bleeds into
> the blue of the sky,
> To fly where the wind alone ventures . . .
> you and I!

The poet closes his book and looks up, blinking away unshed tears. "The poem was written by our Aleksandr Sergeevich Pushkin," he murmurs. "He called it 'Prisoner.'"

The *zeks* around the table tap their spoons on the tin plates by way of applause. The poet, who was celebrated in literary circles before his arrest as an enemy of the people, half rises to his feet and bows from the waist.

When the poet has managed to back down the ladder to his straw pallet, the Greek and his *vory* friend Mikhail "Mika" Rasputin set out the dominoes, fashioned from chips of bone-dry soap, for their nightly game. Rasputin, who is said to be the illegitimate grandson of the murdered monk Rasputin, wears a frayed woolen turtleneck sweater over his cream-colored shirt and has a long matted black beard and a foul temper. He is able to read with his lips sounding out the letters, but he can decipher the coded language of *vory* tattoos fluently. A playing card means the prisoner was sent up for gambling; a dollar sign signifies a safecracker; a dagger into the neck identifies the *zek* as a sex offender. Lice, one of Timur's sixers, the lowest rank in the *vory v zakone* (named for the lowest card in Russian card games), is heating flatirons on the wood-burning stove. Like the other sixers in Timur's band of Ossetes, Lice is assigned household chores when he isn't running errands or providing sex or slitting the throat of someone the *pakhan* has condemned to death. Now he spits on one of the irons to see if it is sizzling hot, then spreads a blanket across the wooden table and begins to iron Timur's long johns. After a bit a guard climbs the ladder to the attic. He glances around, spots Timur, and hands him a folded slip of paper.

Timur opens it, then looks up quickly. "You're positive it's him?"

The guard, offended, squints. "You pay me to be positive about the tips I bring to you."

Timur turns away, conjuring the horizon, where the blue of the sea bleeds, at sunset, into the blue of the sky. The guard pockets the rubles the Greek slips him, and leaves. At a gesture from Timur, two *vory* sixers close the trapdoor behind him and shoulder a large wooden trunk, filled with cartons of canned food and a case of vodka, over it. Timur beckons to his enforcer, Mika Rasputin, who has three skulls tattooed on the backs of three fingers of his right hand, one for each stool pigeon he has strangled. Timur, his lips barely moving, murmurs something to Rasputin, who turns and snaps an order to two of the sixers—Lice and Spare Rib. The three men exchange grim looks. Rasputin makes the sign of the Orthodox cross (even though he is Iron Din, the Ossetes' true faith, on his mother's side), then threads his way between bunks to the far corner of the attic and hauls the prisoner known as Cross-Eyes off his mattress. Lice, an amateur sumo wrestler before he was sent to the penal colony, and Spare Rib, a lean weight lifter, drag him across the floor to Timur and peel his sweater and T-shirt off his back. Stalin's face is tattooed over Cross-Eyes' heart—something *zeks* do in the belief that if they ever face a firing squad the guards will refuse to shoot at the Genius of Humanity—alongside the tiny Ossete *vory* tattoo of Lenin on his right breast.

"*Chukhan!*" Timur hisses, wheezing through his bad nostril. *Stool pigeon.*

Around the attic *zeks*, anticipating theater, sit up in their bunks.

"*Klyanus mamoi,*" Cross-Eyes snivels. "I swear on my mother, it was not me."

Timur nods to Rasputin. The condemned man begs for his life. "My wife's in the women's b-b-barrack . . . They threatened the guards would gang-rape her if I d-d-didn't work for them." His nose runs, mucus collects on his upper lip, his thick canvas trousers darken around the crotch.

Shaking his head angrily, Timur turns away. "Erase his *vory* tattoo," he orders.

Grasping that he has been sentenced to death, Cross-Eyes blurts out defiantly, "*Yob tvoyu mat'*"—*Fuck your mother.*

Rasputin and the sixers drag Cross-Eyes back to his bunk and pin him down. Lice retrieves one of the steaming flatirons from the stove and starts to burn Lenin off the condemned man's breast. Cross-Eyes manages a single excruciating scream before Rasputin presses a pillow onto his face. The condemned man thrashes wildly. After a while his elbows jerk spastically. Then his twitching limbs grow still.

"Sorry, *pakhan*, but he swallowed his pillow," Rasputin announces laconically. "Guess I need to tattoo another skull on my fingers."

The *vory*, watching from their bunks, laugh nervously.

"Fetch the medic at morning sick call," Timur instructs Rasputin. "Tell him someone died of heartburn up here."

Timur, fully clothed—he doesn't remove his leather galoshes at night—stretches out on his bunk, pulls two blankets up to his neck, touches the tip of his thumb to his lips, and then plants the thumb, and the kiss it holds, onto the black-and-white photograph thumbtacked to the wall next to his head, with the words *Roman at his fifth birthday party* written on it in ink.

2
ROMAN:
YOUR SABBATICAL ENDS HERE . . .

MOSCOW

Wednesday, December 25, 1991

The whine of the Tupolev's three engines has been reduced to white noise he no longer hears. Overhead, the *Fasten Seat Belt* sign comes on, with the *lt* in *Belt* flickering as one swept-back wing lifts and the plane curls into its flight path to Sheremetyevo International, north of Moscow. Roman can feel the loss of altitude in his ears. He raises the shade on the oval window. Wispy slivers of cumulus cotton rinse the silver carcass of the Tupolev. The orange disk of the setting sun grazes a distant skyline. The corpulent English businessman sitting next to him shuts his eyes and takes a sweaty grip on the armrest, but Roman, sipping the last of his kvass, is comfortable with the otherworldliness of flying through clouds. In a sense, he has been flying through clouds as far back as he can remember. The left wing dips treacherously and the ground, suddenly visible through the oval window in the fading daylight, rushes up to meet the plane. Deck plates shudder underfoot as the wheel pods groan open. Roman can make out a long line of trucks stalled at a police checkpoint on the Moscow-Petersburg highway. A herd of yellow militia cars stampedes along the access road to the airport, blue roof lights flashing madly, sirens screaming silently. The gray tarmac scarred with skid marks floats up to the plane's wheels and smacks against them once, twice; then the white noise erupts in Roman's head as the Tupolev's engines, originally designed to power Soviet bombers, roar in reverse. The Englishman opens his eyes and manages a wan smile, relieved to still be alive. Some of the passengers applaud, two women sitting across the aisle make the sign of the cross, but Roman does neither.

He is not thrilled to be home.

Inside the airport, he joins the long queue snaking toward passport control. When he reaches the booth, a woman frontier officer with thick-penciled brows and a not-quite-defrosted frown scrutinizes his passport.

"Are you visiting or returning permanently?"

"Returning permanently."

"Remove your sunglasses."

Roman peels them off. The woman's expressionless eyes compare the photograph on the passport to the face in front of her. "What happened to the beard?" she demands.

"A razor happened to the beard."

"You're making a mistake if you think that's humorous."

"I wasn't trying to be humorous. I was trying to be accurate."

The frontier officer checks the angled mirror above Roman's head to be sure he is not making himself shorter or taller than the height listed on the passport. She slams a stamp onto a page of the passport and shoves it back at him through the slot. Roman stops himself from saying thank you; from an early age, Timur drilled into him that *vory v zakone* treat people in uniform with an absolute minimum of courtesy lest they confuse courtesy with respect.

One level down there is an endless wait at the carousel for the baggage to arrive. When the valises finally begin to plunge through the portal onto the carousel, Roman's white duffel bag with *Fleet Chief Petty Officer Wunderly* and *HMS Ceylon* stenciled on it—he bought it for a song at a thrift shop near London's Piccadilly Circus—is one of the first to emerge. Slinging the duffel over his shoulder, he heads down the *Nothing to Declare* lane toward the street door. Just inside it his path is blocked by three men in trench coats. One of them thrusts a laminated identity card in his face. "I don't need to see that," Roman says. "I know a cop when I see one."

"Roman Timurovich Monsurov, son of Timur Monsurov?"

"What game do you play? Why ask my name when you obviously know who I am?"

"You will follow us," the trench coat who appears to be in charge snaps.

"Where are you taking me?"

"You'll know that when we get there."

Roman falls in behind him. The other two trench coats bring up the rear. The English businessman, pushing an enormous suitcase on wheels, recognizes his neighbor from the plane. "I say, old boy, you wouldn't be interested in sharing a . . ." He notices the three trench coats with Roman sandwiched between them and coughs up a bone-dry snicker. "I see you've made other arrangements, sport."

Roman is escorted to an overheated room that reeks of fresh paint and orange peel. A cluster of men, some in civilian suits, some in the uniform of frontier guards, and several female secretaries crowd around the small television sitting on a broken kitchen chair in a corner. "We are now able to confirm that

Mikhail Sergeevich Gorbachev is resigning as general secretary of the Central Committee of the Communist Party as well as Soviet president," the news anchor on the screen announces breathlessly. One of the secretaries gasps, another covers her mouth with the palm of her hand. "Boris Nikolaevich Yeltsin," the announcer plunges on, "the man who led the resistance to the August coup d'état against Gorbachev by misguided Soviet generals and discredited KGB hard-liners, has emerged from the rubble of the Soviet Union as the most powerful political figure in Moscow and the leader of the newly formed Commonwealth of Independent States."

"If you people are addicted to television during office hours," the trench coat who led Roman to the room says, his voice thick with sarcasm, "watch it somewhere else."

"Comrade Ivanov, please, this is the only television around here that works," one of the women explains.

Comrade Ivanov, clearly used to being obeyed, lowers his voice a notch. "If you won't turn that damn thing off, I will!" Reaching down, he yanks the plug out of the wall socket. The television screen goes dark. Muttering under their breath, the men and their secretaries drift out of the room.

One of the trench coats turns Roman's duffel upside down and spills the contents onto a trestle table, then begins to methodically search through his belongings. The chief settles onto the old wooden swivel chair behind the massive standard-issue Soviet desk and motions Roman to the seat facing him. Suspecting he may be here for some time, Roman strips off his RAF-surplus bomber jacket and drapes it over the back of the chair before sitting down. At the trestle table, the trench coat sifting through the contents of the duffel opens a tube of Musgo Real Shave Cream, sniffs at it, then begins squeezing the contents into a crock filled with orange peel.

"In England," Roman remarks nonchalantly, "the border police would be obliged to reimburse me for the shaving cream."

"First, let me correct your mistaken notion that you are in the presence of border police," Comrade Ivanov says. "My colleagues and I work for the Sixth Bureau of the new Organized Crime Control Department in the Ministry of Internal Affairs." He produces a churlish smile that has no ghost of benevolence. "Second, in case it has escaped you, we are not in England here. If you want to recuperate your shaving cream, you are welcome to stuff it back into its tube." He swivels 180 degrees and back as if winding himself up, then leans over the desk and inspects Roman. He takes in the faded jeans, the pale blue shirt with a starched white collar, the belted green sweater with its soft high neck. When Roman glances impatiently at his watch, the interrogator spots the gold Patek Philippe on his left wrist. "What possible use is it to a *vor* to keep track of the phases of the moon?" he asks, his tone logged with scorn.

"Owning a Quantième Perpétuel permits me to feel superior to a *Homo sovieticus* from the Organized Crime Control Department who has a Soviet watch on his wrist that tells the hour—unless, of course, it is overwound, in which case it can be relied on to tell the hour only twice a day."

"It's you who are overwound, my young friend," Comrade Ivanov says coldly. "Be careful how you talk to a *Homo sovieticus* who has done his homework, who knows who you are and where you come from. The sun is at your back, Roman Timurovich. Your shadow precedes you. You turned up on the radar when you swiped a bulletproof Toyota Land Cruiser parked behind the KGB's Lubyanka headquarters and then sold it back to the KGB chief of operations you stole it from."

"I was a kid then—it was a prank."

Comrade Ivanov gestures at the scar over Roman's left ear.

"The Jew who shot at you when your father's Ossetes were battling for control of the river port at Rechnoi Vokzal turned up floating in a cesspit a few days later. The coroner attributed his death to a bullet hole over his left ear—curiously, just where your scar is."

Roman touches the scar with his fingertips. "You're mistaken if you think this is a bullet wound. I tripped in the shower."

"It is rumored that you personally shot the deputy managing director of Moscow's Vnukovo Airport as your initiation into your father's *vory v zakone*."

Roman barely stifles a laugh. "I don't know where you dredged up that story. The managing director owed my father a small fortune. It was a prank designed to scare him into paying his debt. The pistol was loaded with blanks. The heart attack, which was confirmed by the public prosecutor after an autopsy, came as an unpleasant surprise to the deputy managing director. To my father also, I might add. Due to the inconvenient demise of the debtor, the debt was never repaid."

"You're notorious in certain circles for cornering the market on sugar when everyone in Russia was trying to brew moonshine vodka after Gorbachev introduced his *sukhoi zakon*. You weren't a kid then."

"I audited a course at Lomonosov University on the advantages of a free market and was looking for business opportunities. Gorbachev's dry laws seemed to offer one."

"You would have thought, having experienced university life here in Moscow and, more recently, having gotten a taste of life in the mecca of capitalism, London, before being expelled from England by our colleagues at MI5, a smart man in faded designer jeans would put all this *vory v zakone* shit behind him. So, Roman Timurovich, have you returned to Russia to look for more business opportunities?"

"I've returned to Russia because I am Russian."

At the trestle table, Trench Coat begins stuffing Roman's belongings back into the duffel bag. "I am going to do you the favor of not mincing words," Comrade Ivanov announces. "With this alcoholic clown Yeltsin running the show, conditions here will get worse before they get better. The *pakhan* Timur and his Ossete *vory* would be playing with fire if they were to think of the chaos to come as a business opportunity. Deliver that message to your illustrious father."

"Who shall I say signed it?"

The interrogator thrusts himself to his feet, his chin jutting, a forefinger planted on the Communist Party pin on his lapel. "Comrade Boris Ivanov—like his father before him, a *Homo sovieticus.*"

Pushing through the terminal door, Roman is startled by the dry iciness of the Moscow air. Darkness has shrouded the airport; streetlights and head lamps stab through the evening haze. For the span of several heartbeats, he finds breathing difficult. He stops in his tracks, inhaling deeply, only to feel a burning sensation in his lungs. A black Range Rover with tinted windows squeals to a stop at the curb. The passenger door flies open and Mika Rasputin, leaning across from the driver's seat, yells, "Get the fuck in before your balls freeze and fall off."

Roman is only too happy to comply. Flinging his duffel into the back, he climbs in, slamming the door behind him. The Range Rover's heater is running full blast. "I thought you'd never come out," Rasputin grumbles as he throws the car in gear and pulls onto the airport's access road. "I parked in the goddamn three-minute zone. The cops kept coming over and ordering me to move on. Naturally, I didn't. Mikhail Rasputin doesn't take orders from cops. Where the fuck were you?"

"I was having a fascinating conversation with a lemming asking directions to the nearest cliff."

"Lemming have a name?"

"Comrade Ivanov of the Organized Crime Control Department in the Ministry of Internal Affairs."

Mika snorts. "There's a gag going around: If everything is so disorganized in Russia, what with the Soviet Union kaput and the free market exploding, how come crime is so organized?" He snickers at his own joke. "Those clowns in Crime Control are chasing their fucking tails. When Gorbachev blundered onto the scene—Jesus, was that six years ago? Incredible how time flies!—it turned out that his Communist tax collectors weren't collecting enough taxes to pay the state's electric bills, forget salaries. So the esteemed general secretary was obliged to shrink the KGB budget and put some twenty thousand officers out to pasture. Some of those fuckers wound up signing on to these new Organized Crime Control Departments; the others joined more or less legal private protection agencies. Mother Russia, with or without Communists, is a three-ring circus—crime fighters cracking down on *vory* who are competing with private protection agencies staffed by crime fighters."

Roman glances at his longtime friend, twenty years his senior. "Who was it that said it's impossible to govern a country with eleven time zones?"

"Your sainted father is who said it."

Roman catches sight of the four faded skulls tattooed on the fingers of Mika's hand gripping the steering wheel. "You and Timur go back a long way."

"That we do, Roman. We do that."

"What's changed in Russia since I've been in England?"

"Ha! I've changed. I'm in love."

"Again!"

"This time it's for real. I'm in love with this Range Rover. I got promoted. In my previous incarnation, back at Corrective Labor Colony Number Forty, I was Timur's enforcer; now I'm his chief brigadier. My namesake, the monk Rasputin, who used the informal *ty* when chatting up the late Tsar Nicholas, would have been pleased with his illegitimate grandson. Me, Mikhail Rasputin, a fucking brigadier! The promotion comes with a Range Rover, five hundred US a month, and a West German mobile telephone that, unlike our marvelous Soviet phones, actually works as long as you're in the street and remember to open the antenna."

"Salutations, Brigadier Rasputin. I was wondering why you shaved off your lovely tangled beard."

"And I was wondering why you shaved yours off. You look, well, younger without the beard. What did you study in London, my Roman?"

"The English language. The difference between Shakespeare's plays published in the 1604 quarto and the 1623 folio—*Romeo and Juliet*, *King Lear*, *Hamlet*. Pubs. Fish and chips. Guinness on draught. Girls in miniskirts on draught. Especially one girl named Ophelia."

"Ha! That explains the beard," Mika says with a twinkle. "In my not-very-limited experience, some girls don't appreciate a beard tickling their cunts." He laughs at his own joke. "Speaking of cunts, Rosalyn has been phoning every day, wanting to know when you'll be back."

"What did you tell her?"

Mika keeps his eyes on the road. "I may have told her I wasn't sure you were coming back."

"Why did you lie?"

"Look, your father's not thrilled about you seeing—do I *really* need to spell it out?—seeing a Jewish girl. You didn't hear this from me, but that's the real reason he packed you off to London."

"He has not minced words with me the one time the subject was raised."

"What are you going to do?"

Roman stares out the window. After a moment he says, "I'm twenty-six years old, Mika. I'm going to lead my life."

"Your father may have other . . ." Mika doesn't finish the thought.

They drive in silence for a quarter of an hour. Roman glances at his friend. "So tell me, Mika, what does a brigadier do for five hundred US a month?"

Mika is relieved to change the subject. "I do what I've always done, only more so. I'm the honcho of Timur's twenty-three enforcers. I look after your father's business interests. I suss out young Ossetes who could be recruited into our *vory v zakone*. And I watch your ass when Your Holiness honors us with his presence in Moscow."

Roman wipes the condensation off the window with his forearm and gazes at the aurora Moscow projects onto the damp sky. "What else has changed around here?"

"Don't get me started, for fuck's sake. What else has changed? Russia has changed. The shadow economy that drove the fucking Communists up the wall, or should I say *over* the wall, has exploded in their faces. Levi's blue jeans, Nike sneakers, Chanel number something or other are fabricated in grungy garages. Private restaurants are popping up like termites in an apparatchik's dacha. There's a new Georgian eatery across from the Novodevichy graveyard. You need to pay in hard currency, but the wine is French and their flatbreads, stuffed with lamb and onions and grilled over red-hot coals, are mouthwatering. Ha! Just last week some enterprising Armenian *vory* went and opened a casino in a hotel basement. You name it, someone either imports it or manufactures it and sews on a *Made in France* label."

Mika was driving on the highway to Moscow now, weaving in and out of traffic, impatiently flicking his high beams at the car ahead when it didn't get out of his lane fast enough. "The fucking Crime Control comedians haven't stopped our *vory* from providing what the Communist Party is incapable of providing. I'm talking about *krysha.* I'm talking about a *roof* over the heads of those newly minted capitalists opening private businesses so fast Lenin must be squirming in his tomb on Red Square. I'm talking about protection from the Georgian or Armenian or Azerbaijani or Dagestani gangs that run get-rich-quick scams and don't let anything like your father's *vory* code get in their way. I'm talking about protection from the *sportsmen*—the weight lifters and wrestlers who tool around Moscow in Chevrolet pickup trucks with their ridiculous baggy trousers and clean-shaven heads, chewing American gum and flaunting shotguns and Kalashnikovs. They negotiate a *krysha* one day and double the price the next and kill the poor bastard of a capitalist who doesn't pay through the nose. Just last week they buried one alive in a coffin until his wife signed his chain of imported-perfume stores over to them. Why are you smiling? I'm not making this up."

"Okay. I'll make it easier for you. What hasn't changed?"

"That *is* easier. Your sainted father hasn't changed. He's the same stubborn *pakhan* who lives by the code every *vory v zakone* except him thinks is obsolete. Ha! Another thing that hasn't changed is the fucking Communists, what's left of them. They needed us around to parade through Red Square a couple of times a year and fight their fucking war in Afghanistan, but they never gave a flying fuck about the people who did their dirty work."

Roman notices Mika keeping an eye on his rearview mirror. He leans forward, his eyes on the side-view mirror. "Mika, there's a car following us. It's been there since we left the airport."

"Damn right there's a car following us. You're losing your touch, kid—took you long enough to spot it. You don't think I'd deliver you to your father without a backup. It's two of my enforcers—Lice and Spare Rib. When you knew them, they were both sixers. They got themselves promoted too."

Relieved, Roman manages a grin. "Bring me up to speed on the turf war."

"Ah! The Great Moscow Turf War, as our *Pravda* propagandists call it, sells newspapers and keeps Muscovites entertained these days. If anything, the turf war between the different *vory* is hotter than when you left. You'd think a Hollywood filmmaker had turned up in town to shoot a movie about warring mafia godfathers. The Afghanistan veterans organized a bloody *naezd* and took over the gigantic Danilovskii Market from the Azeri. There were so many bodies in the street the police had to send an army truck to collect them. That happened at the beginning of December. Last week the cops found the bodies of three Koptevo gorillas buried in the concrete floor of a sauna. The word on the street is the Chechens get their methods, even their jargon, from American mafia films. Your father has a soft spot for the Chechens. I think it's because, like him, they fought Soviet power."

"No, no, it's because he did time with their *pakhan*, Zaur Zazairov. My father used to say they 'boiled in the same pot.' For Timur, it's all about the *vory* code. As long as the Chechens continue to honor it, my father will honor them."

"The Jew *vory* are Timur's biggest headache. They've gone and recruited thirty, forty new thugs—Jews from Samarkand and Vilnius, a bunch even from Birobidzhan, that Jew oblast

Stalin set up in Siberia, which means they have more mouths to feed, more wallets to fill. All of a sudden their bailiwick that the five *vory* groups agreed on last year when we divided up Moscow isn't big enough for them. Your father can read the handwriting on the wall as well as the next man. The *razborka*, the shootout, with the Jew *vory* is not a matter of *if* but *when*."

Mika guns the Range Rover up a winding road into the Lenin Hills. Roman can make out a crowd of old men and women huddled under the shelter of a bus stop, stamping their feet to keep them from becoming frostbitten. They have set out personal odds and ends on the curb—lamps, mirrors, vases with plastic flowers, handworked kitchen meat grinders, an assortment of musical instruments, winter coats and fur hats and galoshes—and are haggling over the prices with Muscovites waiting for the next bus. "Who are these people?" Roman asks.

"Pensioners. You can find them at subway stations and bus stops all over the city these days. This is what seventy years of fucking Communism has done to Russia. With inflation, their pensions are worthless. They sell what they have to eat one meal a day."

"What do they do when they run out of things to sell?"

Mika looks quickly at his young friend. "They stop eating."

Mika eases the Range Rover up to a high metal gate with the cold-forged initials *VT* interlaced on top and flashes his headlights twice. The gates slowly edge open, and the Range Rover, with the backup car close behind, crawls down the long gravel driveway toward the mansion set well back from the road so that its original owner, the filthy-rich tsarist banker Victor Tuganov, who ended his days in front of a Bolshevik firing squad, would not be disturbed by the sound of traffic.

The Rover pulls to a stop in front of the mansion. One of Timur's *vor*, huddled in an army greatcoat and hood issued to soldiers in the Arctic, can be seen at the top of the petal-shaped staircase, vapor spilling from his mouth, a Kalashnikov cradled in one arm, inspecting the car in the beam of a dazzling flashlight. Mika throws up a hand to shield his eyes. "Forget the duffel," he tells Roman. "I'll have the guard bring it up. Your sabbatical ends here. Your father is expecting you."

3
ROMAN: TRAVEL SAFELY, BUT TRAVEL . . .

LONDON

The backstory

With twenty-twenty hindsight, I suspect that my eyes started itching the moment my feet hit the ground at London City Airport. Forget empirical evidence. My hunch attributed the allergic reaction to the city itself, which, while it obviously doesn't have the majesty of *Muscovy Rus*, is pretty enough if you are someone who finds Macbeth's witches attractive. Seeing the umbrella-armed crowd, with stiff upper lips disfiguring their faces, waiting for the light to change before crossing a street with no traffic only aggravated my newfound allergy. I was accustomed to the casual chaos of Russians, who never wait for a green light, traffic or no traffic, for fear of being mistaken for sheep. Lest I come across as unreasonably negative, I admit to having been pleasantly surprised at being able to breeze past their passport people at the airport. "Russian, are we now?" the ruddy-cheeked Irish cop behind the window remarked as he splashed one of his stamps onto a virgin page in my passport.

"Enjoy your stay, laddie," he said with a suggestive wink of a bloodshot eye.

"I'm counting on doing exactly that," I informed him. Allergy aside, with any luck my exile—ordered up by my sainted father to put twenty-five hundred kilometers between me and my Jewish occasional girlfriend, Rosalyn—would shape up as a prolonged vacation with, hopefully, benefits. (When I thought *benefits*, I had in mind the photographs in *Vogue* of miniskirted birds of a feather patrolling the King's Road.) I'd prepared a cover story for the inevitable interview with MI5 but wound up trying it on for size when I was being sussed out (as the Brits say) by Anthony, eighth Earl of Torthorwitch. I'd turned up, thanks to an ad in the *Guardian*, to rent the one-bedroom flat off the garden of his Belgravia mews house. "I am the only son of a Soviet prisoner"—the best lies are the ones that nibble around the edge of truth—"who, on his release from the gulag, scrimped for years to send me to London," I explained. "Do you understand *gulag*, Anthony?"

"Rings a bell," Anthony, who was roughly my age, allowed. "Book on geography by that Solzhenitsyn chap, wasn't it? Something about an archipelago someplace or other. Look, if you're still chuffed after seeing the gammy postage stamp of a weed-ridden garden, flat's yours. When my mates discover I have a genuine Russian living under my roof, they'll be keen to meet you. For us Brits, Russia is the dark side of the moon. When you're settled, do come topside for a six o'clock pick-me-up, old boy."

Anthony's six o'clock pick-me-up, three fingers of a sixteen-year-old Laphroaig lovingly spilled over a single ice cube, picked me up and then some. "So what is it you do?" fortified by Laphroaig, I worked up my nerve to inquire.

My question appeared to amuse Anthony. "Not sure I follow you, old boy. What is it I do where?"

"What is it you do by way of work?"

"Bloody hell, *work*! 'Fraid you'd ask. Chaps like me don't actually work, as in labor in the pound-sterling mines of what we call the City. Not my bag, I'm glad to say. I look after the nest egg my late lamented paterfamilias, the seventh earl, bequeathed me, the nest egg being the chicken feed left after the Revenue wankers helped themselves despite not having been mentioned in the seventh earl's last will and testament. I'm speaking relatively when I say chicken feed, *ça va sans dire*. When I'm not cloistered with dodgy financial blokes trying to convince me to buy short or sell long or some such, I fly. Literally. I am the proud owner and pilot of a swish nosewheel Cessna 172 Skyhawk. Bloody thing was spanking new in 1956; you need to fiddle with the choke to get the engine to turn over, which it does nine times out of ten. Weekends I bobble off to Paris or Amsterdam or Dublin. Been as far as Prague, planning a spree to Vilnius in the Baltics when I've figured out how the bloody radio beacon navigation thingummy works. Off to Barcelona weekend after next with a chum. If you are not previously engaged, come along for the ride."

Which is how I got to meet Anthony's chum named Ophelia.

Ophelia: Tilting her head onto an ironing board (I swear I saw her do this when I woke up in her bedroom the morning after), she managed to iron out the curls so that her silky blond hair hung straight down to the nipples of her lovely breasts. Long bare legs, even in the dead of winter, scuffed lace-up ankle boots advertising her working-class roots, a short midthigh pea-green miniskirt advertising her mindset toward consensual sex, a ribbed body-hugging charcoal-black sweater advertising her feminist's disdain for undergarments. She came armed with a twenty-eight-blade knife and a passion for the actor she called Willy Shake Shaft—that and world revolution. As someone born and raised in a country mutilated by world revolution, I need to admit we didn't exactly hit it off at first sight. She was reasonably impressed by my being Russian but unreasonably depressed by my being, like my sainted father, a dyed-in-the-wool anti-Communist. "What is it about Communism that rubs you the wrong way?" she shouted into my ear as we flew in Anthony's Cessna across the channel in what I hoped was the general direction of Barcelona's airport.

"What is it about Communism that could possibly attract you?" I shouted back.

"Trotsky."

"Trotsky, as in Leon Trotsky!" Here I was, a Russian who had made his way to England for a prolonged vacation with benefits, and who did I wind up sitting next to? Probably the last person on planet Earth who still carried a torch for Lev Bronstein, alias Leon Trotsky. "Jesus, what have you been smoking?" I couldn't resist shouting into her ear.

"Fuck you!" she hollered.

I was pleasantly surprised to find her breath on my ear faintly erotic.

"Fuck me," I agreed.

"What snail shell have you crawled out of?" she shouted. When she saw I didn't understand her question, she rephrased it in the King's English. "Where are you from?"

"My roots are Ossetian. Ossetia is in Georgia. When I last looked, Georgia was unfortunately still in Russia."

"Okay, here's the thing—Tolstoy and company aside, before Lenin and his Bolsheviks came on the scene and changed the world, name one thing Russians contributed to Western civilization."

"The solar year," I shouted.

"The solar year? What have *you* been smoking?"

I fingered a handful of blond hair away from her ear, the better to hear me. "A fellow named Ulugh Beg, he was a grandson of Tamerlane—you've heard of Tamerlane, I suppose?—dug a long trench and, observing the shadow of the sun at high noon, calculated the solar year at three hundred sixty-five days, five hours, forty-nine minutes, and fifteen seconds. He was off by twenty-five seconds."

"So what you're saying is he got it wrong?"

"That was in fourteen hundred something, for Christ's sake."

What worried me was the possibility that Anthony, navigating by the seat of his Savile Row trousers, would run out of gas before he came across a runway to land on; that we would crash into the endless carpet of greenhouses stifling the Spanish countryscape and transforming the ground into reflected sky; that I might perish alongside a decently pretty young female who didn't wear undergarments and was a dying breed—an incurable Trotskyist flaunting her terminal infection. *Workers of the world, get your act together. Forget chains—you have nothing to lose but your goddamn lives!*

Circling the cloud cover obscuring Barcelona, Anthony, thank goodness, spotted an Iberia jetliner off to port and, on the assumption the Spanish pilot knew where he was going, followed in its slipstream, which is how he managed to set his Cessna down on the tarmacadam just as the dial on his gas gauge juddered onto red. "Crikey, bit of a sticky wicket, that," he said with a nervous giggle as he unstrapped his seat belt.

"As Willy Shake Shaft put it in the comedy he swiped from Boccaccio, all's well that ends well," Ophelia said, aiming an edgy half-smirk in my direction.

After depositing our valises in a small hotel on the heights above the city, we wound up at a tapas bar off the Ramblas. "So, exactly what is it about the late and little-lamented Trotsky that you could possibly admire?" I asked Ophelia.

"You're very direct."

"I often talk first and think afterward. My sainted father considers it a fault. My occasional girlfriend, Rosalyn, understands it as me being spontaneous."

"What sometimes passes for spontaneity could be the first sign of foot-in-mouth disease. As for Trotsky, to answer your spontaneous question, to his dying day he preached a religion he called 'permanent revolution.' Trotsky saw the Bolshevik Revolution as the beginning, not the end. He was convinced that the old man, Lenin, and his revolution wouldn't survive without a sister revolution in Germany or Italy or France or England. Fact is, absent a sister revolution—somewhere, anywhere, fuck, *everywhere!*—your bloody Bolsheviks have a lot in common with lemmings asking directions to the nearest cliff." She dipped a thumb into the lobster sauce and, sticking it into her mouth, sucked on it. The gesture took ten years off her biological age and added incrementally to her sex appeal. "If Trotsky had taken over instead of Stalin on Lenin's death," she went on, "he wouldn't have been as brutal as Stalin and Russia wouldn't have suffered as much. Not to mention that the Communist experiment that began in Russia in 1917 might have had a longer shelf life."

I made the blunder of trying to set straight someone who thought the shortest distance between two points was a meandering line. "Your hero Trotsky was enthusiastic about the Red Terror," I informed her. "Your hero Trotsky was all for the collectivization of agriculture, which wound up killing millions. Your hero Trotsky ordained that if tsarist officers serving in his new Red Army betrayed the Bolsheviks, their wives and children would be shot. How in hell can any sane person call themselves a Trotskyite? Your hero Trotsky restored the death penalty and used it ruthlessly. During the civil war that followed the revolution, Commissar of the Army Trotsky would turn up at the front in an armored train, and if a Red division had retreated when the Whites attacked, he would order every tenth soldier to take one step forward and summarily execute them."

"Well, you can bet, thanks to Comrade Trotsky, the soldiers who were still alive didn't retreat again," Ophelia remarked with a smirk. "Thanks to Comrade Trotsky, the Reds won the civil war."

"You're probably not familiar with Trotsky's opinion of the guillotine. He said something about how the French Revolution owed its success to the machine that made the enemies of the people shorter by a head. He considered the guillotine to be a brilliant invention. He thought every Russian city needed one. 'Heads must roll' is what he said."

"He wasn't wrong."

"What do you do, Ophelia, when you're not shilling for Leon Trotsky?"

She almost laughed. "I shill for a bloke named Willy Shake Shaft, as the bard from Stratford-upon-Avon was sometimes called. I teach a graduate seminar at King's College London on the three versions of *Hamlet*."

"Ah. We Russians have had a long love affair with Shakespeare's Danish prince. Schoolchildren memorize the poem Pasternak wrote called 'Hamlet.' Our Grigori Kozintsev filmed a haunting Russian-language *Hamlet*—it was based on a Pasternak translation. Shostakovich composed the film's music. Hey, I didn't know there were three versions of Shakespeare's *Hamlet*."

"There's one version—it may have been Willy's first draft—in the 1603 bad quarto. There's another *Hamlet* in the 1604 good quarto, which is two hundred thirty lines longer than the *Hamlet* in the 1623 folio."

"Who cut these lines in the 1623 folio?"

"Though he was long dead and buried, there's a good chance it was Willy himself. The folio version may have been set in type from Shake Shaft's original stage script of the play. Nobody knows for sure. To cut or not to cut, that is the question."

"Your Trotsky and your Hamlet are not only centuries but also worlds apart."

"Not so," she said flatly. "They have something in common. Trotsky, like Hamlet, was both the avenger and the target of revenge. In Hamlet's case, avenger for his uncle's murder of his father, the king of Denmark; the target of revenge for Hamlet's murder of Laertes's father, Polonius. An echo of Trotsky, you do see it? Trotsky, with his *heads must roll*, was avenging the crimes of centuries of tsars against the masses of the Russian people. He ended his life the target of revenge, with an ice ax planted in his skull on Stalin's orders."

"You ought to teach a course in the three versions of history," I suggested.

She detected the sarcasm in my tone and favored me with the middle finger of her left hand.

The next afternoon, Anthony, who seemed to know the city like the palm of his hand, shepherded us to Barcelona's Plaza de Toros Monumental. We wound up with seats on the sunny side of the bull ring and rented two cushions each—one to sit on, one to hold over our heads to keep the sun out of our eyes. The cries of "¡Olé! ¡Olé!" reverberating through the arena made it difficult to hear myself think, much less pick up where I'd left off with this pretty blond *Hamlet* professor, Ophelia. The matador, who Anthony said was the rage of the *corrida* circuit for restoring long-abandoned passes like the *larga afarolada*, brought the crowd to its feet with a series of more classical *verónicas* that left the poor bull's blood, drawn by the *banderillas*, staining the vest of his suit of lights. When the horses came to drag the bull's now-earless corpse from the arena, Ophelia took advantage of the quiet to tell me, "There is a corner of the *corrida* where, for some crazy reason, the bull feels safe from the madding mob cheering on the matador to kill him. The Spanish have a name for this sanctuary—they call it the *querencia*, literally, the haunt. When you think about it, Trotsky was doing pretty much the same thing: trying to create a haunt that would be a sanctuary for the workers and peasants exploited for centuries by tsars and filthy-rich landlords."

"So your famous—or should I say *infamous*—dictatorship of the proletariat is actually a *querencia* in a Spanish *plaza de toros*?"

"*Querencia* is a metaphor. Hegel tells us that seen from shoe level, capitalist history is a *Schlachtbank*: a slaughterhouse. When the working class throws off its capitalist chains, the dictatorship of the proletariat will be a sanctuary—a place unscarred by imperial wars, class cruelties, and crippling poverty."

"And if such a place existed, would you move there with your copies of the bad and good quartos and the 1623 folio and educate the peasants and factory workers on the three versions of *Hamlet*?"

The smile vanished from Ophelia's lips. "You're trying to take the piss out of me. Mayakovski used to read his poems to factory workers in train stations so icy he said the frost scorched his feet. To answer your question, sure, I'd move to a proletariats' sanctuary in the blink of an eye if one existed. I'd lecture illiterate peasants on the textual differences between the 1603 and '04 quartos and the 1623 folio if I thought it would help the revolution."

"Mayakovski committed suicide when he came to understand that the Union of Soviet Socialist Republics he had helped create wasn't a *querencia*, that Communism, at its heart, is a palimpsest—Bolshevik bullshit superimposed on tsarist horse-shit."

"Fuck you, Roman."

"Fuck me," I cheerfully agreed.

And despite my terminal anti-Communism, she did. Fuck me. That very night. In a narrow bed on the top floor of the Barcelona hotel, with nylon sheets on the spongy mattress and the Virgin Mary gaping down at us from the wall, a frown of chaste discomfort frozen on her pale face. "This is the first time I've slept with a Communist," I told her when we both had quenched our thirst.

"You weren't asleep," she teased. Her eyes turned serious. "First time for me too—never fucked an anti-Communist before."

Two months or so after we'd gotten back to London, Anthony invited me up for another three fingers of his sixteen-year-old Laphroaig. "Been shagging the nutter Ophelia, have you?" he asked casually.

"My private life is private, Anthony. She did haul me off to see Mel Gibson play *Hamlet* in the new Zeffirelli film. They were using a revised text that she had a hand in—something to do with the 1623 folio." And I came up with Hamlet's line that, curiously, had lodged like a splinter in my brain. "From this time forth, my thoughts be bloody."

"Your Ophelia is too highbrow by half for my taste."

"She has a deliciously low lowbrow side, Anthony."

He offered up a very English smirk, which was half-smile, half-leer. "Jammy Russian bastard."

We'd barely gotten past the first two fingers when he cleared his throat as if he anticipated delivering some unpleasant news. "Spit it out," I said, thinking he was going to raise the rent on me.

"Some blokes from our MI5 came sucking round asking

about you this morning," he told me. "Be you a Commie spy or some such?"

"If I were a spy I wouldn't tell you, would I?"

"Hadn't thought of it quite like that."

"For what it's worth, I have, like most males, what Dostoyevsky called 'various little itches,' but spying for Comrade Stalin's Communists is not one of them, Anthony. My father spent twenty-two years in Stalin's gulag. He detests the Communists. The enemy of the father is the enemy of his son."

"Chalk and cheese, you being a spy. Told the bloody MI5 wankers you were the opposite of a spy, though come to think of it I'd be hard put to say what the opposite of a spy is actually. Whatever. I think they think anybody who comes from the far side of the Iron Curtain must be dodgy. Forget they came by. Forget I asked. Down the hatch!"

I would have followed Anthony's advice and forgotten the "blokes from MI5"—I would gladly have gone on with my endless one-night stands with the Trotskyist *querencia* aficionada Ophelia—if they hadn't shown up a few days later for an encore. "You Mr. Monsurov?" said the bloke who came up behind me as I was fitting my key into Anthony's door.

I turned to find three young men in three-piece suits sizing me up. They weren't smiling, which gave me the uncomfortable feeling they didn't like what they saw. "What can I do for you?" I inquired.

"You can leave the country for us," the one with sideburns spilling down his cheeks replied with what I took to be an Irish accent.

"We don't want to rush you," a second bloke said. "You have twenty-four hours to tie up loose ends."

"You want to tell me why I'm being expelled from England?"

"No," the third bloke said pleasantly. "It's a state secret."

"Won't hurt to tell him," the second bloke allowed.

"British mafia isn't happy with Russian mafia pussyfooting around in the Queen's England."

"Is there a British mafia?" I asked.

"Is there a Russian mafia?" Sideburns shot back.

"Beats me," I said. "You don't happen to have an expulsion order in writing that I might see?"

"That's correct. We don't," the second bloke said.

"Hard cheese," the third bloke said.

"Travel safely," Sideburns said, "but travel."

Which is how I came to find myself on a Moscow-bound Tupolev drinking warm kvass next to a corpulent English businessman who, fearful of flying in a heavier-than-air silver cigar, kept his eyes shut tight for most of the flight home.

4
ROMAN: WE ARE ON THE WRONG SIDE OF HISTORY . . .

MOSCOW

Back to the frontstory

Returning to his father's mansion stuck to the flypaper skyline on the Lenin Hills, with Mikhail "Mika" Rasputin throwing open the great front doors ahead of him, Roman is suddenly swept up in a cataract of remembrances: the tumult of the ground-floor rooms swarming with people he had never seen before, a ragtag collection of women and men, some of whom hadn't bathed in weeks—or eaten in days—come to beg favors from his father. Even now, meandering through the empty rooms, he can visualize the boy who desperately wanted to get out of the Red Army, the girl who threatened to kill herself if she couldn't get out of an arranged marriage, the young woman shrouded in moth-eaten furs who was prepared to sleep with the devil for a part in a Konchalovsky film. Roman has been making his way through the ground-floor rooms as far back as he can remember, navigating past worn army rucksacks and *avoskas* filled with oranges and ashtrays overfull of cigarette ends and babies crawling on the threadbare carpet strewn with the husks of sunflower seeds. Even with the rooms deserted, in his mind's ear he can still hear raddled women coughing and sobbing; in his mind's eye he can still see unshaven men squirming and groveling.

"Why are these people always here?" he once asked his father.

Timur avoided his eye. "They are hoping I can give them something that the Communists can't—or won't," he answered.

"And can you?"

"Depending on what they can do for me in return, at times yes."

Roman starts up the back stairway, past the framed photos of the towns and cities Timur lingered in during his eight-month trek across the Urals thirty-eight years before: Tobolsk Kremlin; Tyumen with its hot springs; Chelyabinsk; Perm, on the Kama River's salt flats; Ufa; Yekaterinburg, where the Bolsheviks executed the tsar Nicholas, along with his German-born wife and their five children. The second-floor dining room was the scene of Roman's earliest memory: his fifth birthday party (though he was never sure whether he actually remembered it or had seen the photograph on the wall of the dining room so often he *imagined* remembering it). In the grainy black-and-white photograph, a dozen or so children could be seen sitting around the massive dining-room table, their parents standing sentinel behind them, servants in white dinner jackets hovering behind the parents, and Roman, with the telltale pout disfiguring his cherubic face, presiding at the head of the table. One person was conspicuously missing from the photograph: Timur. Roman's Ossete nanny, hoping to explain Timur's absence to her young charge, would tell him his father was a very important man, the equivalent of a commissar, in charge of many men stationed in a remote Soviet base doing top-secret work for the motherland. All of which turned out to be *almost* true: He was the *pakhan* of the thirty-eight *vory v zakone* in Corrective Labor Colony No. 40—a detail Roman only discovered when he was a teenager and Mika, quite drunk one night, let slip that he had done time with his father.

"Done time how?" Roman, unfamiliar with the expression, asked.

"There's only one way to *do* time in the Soviet Union, boy—that's in a Soviet prison."

Watching Timur across the dining-room table the next day, Roman saw his father in a new light: the notched features that remained expressionless when one of his brigadiers questioned a decision, the narrowed eyes that always seemed to be listening to what you weren't putting into words, the gray hair cropped so short the maplike blotches on his scalp were visible, the faded blue tattoos on the backs of three fingers of his left hand—three tiny onion-shaped domes draped in barbed wire signifying, as Mika explained to Roman, that his father was a *vozhd*, a guide.

"And whom does he guide?"

"You ask too many questions, kid."

"Do you say that because you don't know the answer?"

"I say that because you won't understand the answer."

In time, Roman came to know the answer. And to understand it.

Making his way up to the third floor, Roman notices the framed photograph of the white bell tower in the Saint Nicholas the Miracle Worker monastery in the town of Dzerzhinskiy, a half hour distant from Moscow. He is suddenly swamped with remembrances of the time Timur, days after returning from the remote Soviet base, kept him out of school to take him on an expedition. "And where are we going, my father?" he remembers asking as the four-door Volga, with one of the Ossete sixers at the wheel, made its way along Volgogradskiy Prospekt.

"We are off to Siberia, my son," Timur had replied, his face creased into a rare smile.

Roman, eleven at the time and wearing laced high shoes and baggy knee-length knickerbockers, was thrilled to be going to Siberia with his father. He thought of the stories he could tell his schoolmates when he got back. Roman remembers trudging up the steel steps of the bell tower behind Timur, pulling himself along by the steel banister, calling to his father one landing above him, "And have you ever been to Siberia?"

Even now, looking at the photograph of the bell tower in the stairwell of the tsarist banker's mansion, Roman can make out Timur's slightly breathless voice wafting down to him. "I have spent a bit of time in Siberia, my son."

"At a secret remote base?"

"The base was secret and remote, yes."

"And is it as cold as they say in my geography book?"

"Colder still," Timur called over his shoulder. "In the winter even vodka freezes, instead of drinking it you suck on vodka icicles. If you cry, the tears freeze on your face before they can fall to the ground." Reaching the top level of the bell tower, immediately under the golden dome, Timur educated his son. "You are in the tallest monastery bell tower in all of Russia. From here, so it is said, it is possible to see Siberia. Climb onto this milk crate and tell me what you see."

"I see only forest, Father."

"Look again, my darling son. Look through the trees, look past the forest, and tell me what you see."

Roman, eager to please Timur, remembers inventing a Siberia: "Oh boy, I see a great frozen steppe, Father. I see white polar bears struggling through knee-deep snow. I see a mother fox snuggling with her babies in a nest of leaves and twigs to keep them warm."

"Well done, my son. From now on, if anybody asks, you can say you have experienced Siberia."

Opening the door to his father's private apartment, Roman spots the *vozhd* standing with his back toward him, holding a sheaf of paper up to the light of a lamp. The sight of his surprisingly frail, slightly stooped father reading something with a magnifying glass moves Roman to tears, which, thankfully, freeze in his eyes before they can fall to the ground. Hearing someone at the door, Timur turns his head, gasps, then shuffles past the cart laden with zakuski to fold his son into an awkward embrace. "Welcome back to Mother Russia," he murmurs. "Welcome back to Moscow. Welcome home."

Timur, his gray hair cut short in the style of sailors, the round bifocals Roman sent him from London slipping down his broken nose, drops ice cubes into two wineglasses, swirls them by their stems to ice the glass, then half fills them with vodka. He hands one to Roman and hikes his glass to offer up a toast. "*Na nashe zdorov'ye*, my darling son. To our health!"

"*Na tvoe zdorov'ye*, my dear father. To *your* health!"

Roman's *tvoe* brings a half-smile to Timur's lips. "I have never traveled on an airplane," he remarks, "but I have been told by some who have that fear of flying increases appetite. If this is true, you will be hungry," he adds, waving toward the Baltic herring, the Caspian caviar, the wedges of Arctic salmon, the marinated radishes. "Eat up, eat your fill. And then tell me what it was like to spend three months living abroad." He motions Roman to a leather couch and draws up a chair facing him.

"I missed your birthday," Roman says. "How does it feel to be seventy-four?"

"It feels inconvenient. When I do the arithmetic, I realize I have lost almost twenty-five years of my life sleeping."

"Did you lose eight hours a day sleeping in prison?"

"In prison, I lost sixteen hours a day being awake."

The father, wearing a dark double-breasted suit jacket and trousers that may have had a crease in a previous incarnation, and his son, in faded jeans and a belted green sweater, make small talk until they run out of it. All the while Timur chain-smokes American Camels, lighting a new one from the glowing ashes of its predecessor as if making up for all the cigarettes he never smoked in prison. After a time, the silence becomes as thick as the cigarette smoke in the room. Clearing his throat, Roman waves a hand to scatter the smoke and breaks a silence that has become awkward. "Father, there is something . . ." He takes a breath and starts again. "Something I've been working up the nerve to say to you for years: You never speak of my mother."

"You never ask about your mother."

"I'm asking now."

"She was a nurse . . ."

"I know that. Were you married?"

"We were more than married when she gave me what my heart came to desire more than life itself: a son."

"When she died, did you grieve?"

Timur turns to stare at his own reflection in the darkened window. "The thing I like least about this house is you don't hear the sound of traffic rising up from the city. I miss the sound of traffic. It tells me where I am. Knowing where I am reminds me of where I'm *not*—Strict Regime Corrective Labor Colony Number Forty—and how far I have journeyed from my Georgian village, Areshperani, to get here." He turns his back on the reflection in the window. "Sorry, sorry. What were you saying?"

"Did you grieve when my mother died?"

"I grieved when I found the Ossete meat pie she had prepared so I would have something to eat while she was in the hospital."

"Why was she in the hospital? Was she sick?"

Timur refills the two glasses with vodka. "Let's not spoil your first night home. We will speak of this another time." He half smiles as he changes the subject. "What did you learn in the capitalist city of London that can be instructive to an old *vor* living in the Communist city of Moscow?"

Roman begins talking before he has thought through what he wants to say. "I learned, Father, that we are on the wrong side of history. I learned that our *vory v zakone* must change our ways or perish."

He can't help but notice his father's eyes narrow. He understands this to mean that Timur is listening to what isn't being put into words. Roman hears him say, so quietly he has to strain to catch his words, "You will want to explain that."

Roman runs his finger around the rim of his glass, producing a soft hum, and looks up. "I read books and articles in London on the Great Turf War in Russia that aren't published here, Father. The English, the Americans, are obsessed with what they call the Russian mafia. They think this nonstate enterprise of ours will last a few years at most—what they're already calling the roaring nineties. But the long view is that the post-Soviet state, whether under this Yeltsin character or the rising star in Petrograd, that KGB officer Putin, will eventually put down roots and begin to supply what a state is supposed to supply, which are courts, judges, justice. In short, security. The new state will write new laws and then, in its infinite wisdom, decide who is operating inside the law and destroy those operating outside. It will collect taxes to pay for the security everyone craves. Protection—providing a *roof*—will be a relic from the past once the post-Soviet state gets back into the business of protecting businesses and adjudicating disputes in their *arbitrazh* courts. At which point our *vory* will be like the Neanderthals studied by anthropologists—primitives in sheepskins fighting for the scraps the dinosaur we call the state drops from the table."

Concentrating on his cigarette, slowly shaking his head, Timur digests what his son has told him. "This is what I think," he finally says. "You have landed from another planet. Still, you are my son. I respect you even when I don't agree with you."

"You are my father, still. I honor you."

"That is as it should be."

"The other planet I come from is London, England, Father, where nostalgia for the past—when the sun never set on the British Empire—has given way to a reality check about the future."

"The mistake you make, the miscalculation at the heart of what you say, is thinking the past is past," Timur says. A slight whistle seeps from the nostril of his broken nose. "This future state of yours will never put down roots after Gorbachev's blunder. I am not talking about his lamentable perestroika that brought the seventy-year-old Soviet Union to its knees; I'm talking about his 1989 blunder permitting the Berlin Wall to be dismantled. I'm talking about his opening the door to a unified Germany. The Europeans counted on the now-embalmed Soviet dinosaur to keep Germany fragmented. For those of us for whom the past is *not* past, even two Germanys were not sufficient fragmentation. My God, a unified Germany at the heart of Europe will be like one of those black holes that people much smarter than me think are out there in the vastness of the universe . . ." Timur turns to gaze at the window, not at his reflection in it but *out* the window. "Sucking up everything around it, sucking up the stars and the planets and even the light, which, so they say, is why we don't see these black holes. Once a single black hole forms anywhere in the cosmos, the fate of the rest of the universe is sealed. It may take an eternity, but there will be no escaping it." Turning back to Roman, Timur, exasperated, shrugs one shoulder. "A post-Soviet state putting down roots in the foreseeable future! It will never happen, my darling son from another planet called London. Here, for what it's worth, is how your father sees the future: Russia will be reduced to an economic vassal of this reconstituted Germany in the heart of Europe, a black hole of a country sucking up everything around it."

Mika joins them in the room and hands Timur the evening newspaper. He glances at the headline trumpeting the arrival of Boris Yeltsin at the summit of the post-Soviet state, snickers in derision as he drops the newspaper on the floor.

Roman takes in the headlines. "It can be enlightening to step back and see Russia from the distance of another planet, Father," he persists. "The Soviet state and its policing organs withered away, and our *vory* stepped in to fill the void. So far, so good. But we need to turn the page. We need to look ahead and not back. We need to negotiate an amnesty for earlier crimes in return for future obedience to the new state and its new laws."

Mika settles onto the couch next to Roman. "Consider the possibility that he is onto something, *pakhan*. In some cities, the *vory* are falling over each other negotiating amnesty."

Timur produces a bitter grimace. "Amnesty," he cries—the whistle from his bad nostril becomes more distinct—"didn't turn out so well for the *vory* who had the roof at the Vyborg Paper Factory, did it? It didn't turn out so well for the *vory* protecting the Lomonosov Porcelain Factory in Petersburg or the Kachkanar Mining Plant in the Urals. They negotiated one of your famous guarantees against prosecution only to be sent to prison on trumped-up tax-evasion charges. When the so-called tax inspectors turned up unannounced at Abramovich's oil giant, Sibneft, it was nothing short of a *naezd*. The assault began at dawn and lasted into nightfall. Before they left, they smashed every typewriter, every telephone, every mimeograph machine, and for good measure they broke the wrists of anyone who tried to stop them."

"Father, your namesake, Timur the Lame, adapted to new military realities, which is how he managed, against all odds, to defeat the Christian knights at Smyrna. Our *vory* also need to adapt to new realities. With or without amnesty, we need to join the new capitalists. We should get out of the business of providing a roof. We should get into the business of business. Instead of milking businesses, we ought to sit on the boards of directors. We ought to hire accountants and lawyers who know how to keep track of the profits."

Timur, tiring of the conversation, pushes himself to his feet and starts toward the door, then suddenly twists back, eyes pinched, brow furrowed, lips distorted into a sneer. "Is that how you see me, a *vory pakhan*? Sitting in an office crawling with lawyers and accountants in three-piece suits, for God's sake! This new capitalism you would have us join is every bit as decrepit as the old Communism—some have more than they need, most need more than they have. What has changed? I dread that these new realities you would have us adapt to will corrode our thieves' honor, which is all that stood between us and seventy years of Bolshevik brutality. I speak from bitter experience. I spent twenty-two years in their miserable camps."

"Almost as many as Mandela," Roman mutters, but his father, caught up in the web of his rage, doesn't hear him and rushes on.

"There were winters when the only thing we had to eat was snow. There were summers when dried locusts were considered a luxury. Our *vory* existed before the Bolsheviks murdered the tsar, but our honor code was born in Stalin's godforsaken gulags. Living by an honor code is how I survived. It is whispered about that I am nostalgic when it comes to the *vory v zakone*." Timur, squinting, looks hard at his brigadier. "You delude yourself if you think I don't hear it, Mika. It is said I am trapped in the past, a relic of disorganized crime. They are not misreading the tea leaves. These muscle-bound *sportsmeny*, the thousands of unemployed KGB officers staffing the so-called *legal* protection agencies, the new breed of *vory*—the Afghan war veterans with their wounded limbs and wounded pride, the Ingush who will do anything to screw Stalin though his rotting corpse has long since been devoured by maggots, most of all the Jews hungry for revenge on the world for spitting on them for two thousand years—they all have a common obsession. The only thing they respect is force; therefore the only thing they project is force. Their preferred method is *bespredel*—no holds barred: violence for violence's sake, violence for violence's pleasure, violence for a quick adrenaline fix. They are addicted to this adrenaline. They have something else in common: They think my thieves' world is a fossil from some prehistoric excavation."

"Who is to say they are wrong, Father?"

"*I* am here to say they are wrong, my darling son."

There is another of the strained silences that Roman remembers so well from the rare meals he was invited to take with Timur when his father returned, so the boy was told, from the remote base where he did top-secret work for the motherland.

"My watch is still set to Greenwich mean time, Father. Could you tell me the time?"

Mika tugs a very large timepiece from his pocket. "It's—"

"I asked my father."

"You want to know the time where?" Timur asks.

"Here."

Timur stabs his tattooed fingers out of a cuff and glances at his wristwatch. "I don't keep track of the time here," he announces. "In Areshperani, it is ten minutes past midnight."

5
ROSALYN: WHAT THE HELL DID YOU SAY TO MAKE HER ANGRY . . .

MOSCOW

Thursday, January 2, 1992

"I thought you'd never call, Roman."

"How did you know I was in Moscow?"

"That obnoxious bodyguard of yours, that Rasputin person, told me he wasn't sure you were coming back. Which meant you were back."

Rosalyn's laugh is contagious. Roman laughs with her. The laugh gives way to awkward smiles. When the smiles melt away, they kiss on the lips that smiled.

In bed later, Rosalyn lights a joint from the flame on the candle, inhales, passes it to Roman, who sucks on the cigarette several times before handing it back. "Don't take what I'm going to say the wrong way, Roman, but you were focused on something besides me when we made love just now."

"What's the right way to take that?"

Rosalyn tosses a shoulder. "The speed with which you went about producing orgasms—mine first, then yours hard on its heels—Christ, Roman, you'd have thought we were making love in a rented bed, the sooner we finished, the cheaper the tab. Knowing you, knowing how you see sex as a slow-motion ballet, I'd guess you are stressed out. Actually, *stressed out* doesn't begin to describe you. You're as taut as a piano wire. You made love the way someone gasps for air. Being back in Moscow doesn't explain it. Shaving off your lovely beard doesn't explain it. If the past is any indication, you're stressed out by your father."

"The past is never past," Roman remarks.

"The past can be kept bottled up if you concentrate on the present—on the stark-naked body immediately under your stark-naked body."

He reaches for the joint and takes a long drag, holding his breath. "I spent a few days in Barcelona when I was in London. A friend who pilots his own plane took me along for the ride. I wound up in the *plaza de toros* on a Sunday afternoon. In the *corrida*, there is a corner of the arena where for some crazy reason the bull feels protected from the madness around him. The Spanish call it *querencia*. That's what your apartment is to me."

"Jesus, Roman, I wanted my apartment to be more to you than a safe corner of the arena." She turns away and says in a whisper, "I wanted to be more to you than an occasional girlfriend."

Her directness embarrasses Roman. He smiles nervously to cover his embarrassment. "You are more than an occasional girlfriend, Rosalyn. I promise you. Coming home has not been easy. My father expects a lot from me. I don't know if . . . I'm not sure if I can live up to his expectations. I don't know if I can become the man he thinks I must be to be a man." A dark thought clouds his eyes. "I don't want to become the man I'm afraid of becoming."

"You're an apple that has fallen far from the tree," Rosalyn observes.

"I'm an apple that hasn't fallen from the tree. Yet." He touches her bare shoulder. "What can I do to make it up to you?"

"You can take me ice-skating, which, should it have slipped your stressed mind, is how we met."

"I haven't forgotten. I was charmed by your—"

"By my skating, I know."

Roman laughs again. "By your skating, among other things."

Mika drives them to Gorky Park in his Range Rover. "I'll sit in the car, thank you," he announces, turning the heat up a notch. Rosalyn laces up her skates, and she and Roman make their way past the fires flaring in metal drums, to the edge of the pond. "Be sure to watch me," Rosalyn says as she removes the rubber blade caps and leaps onto the frozen pond. Despite the iciness of the night—or because of it; iciness tends to bring Muscovites out after dark—the Gorky pond is packed with skaters: couples in lockstep, with their arms twined around each other, making lazy tours of the rink; half a dozen young men who are clearly professionals, performing acrobatic leaps and twists at one end of the pond; one tall girl in coal-black tights and a short fiery-red skirt who spins so rapidly, her long hair flailing, she has transformed herself into a blur. Loudspeakers fixed to the tops of telephone poles blast an orchestral version of Prokofiev's *Romeo and Juliet* into the night. Women wearing padded ankle-length coats, their heads enveloped in woolen babushkas, peddle hot wine in thermos bottles, ten rubles a glass. Roman, sitting on a wooden bench near one of the fires, sips his steaming-hot wine as he watches Rosalyn, dodging the slower skaters, make several effortless turns around the rink. She skates over to the blur in the middle, who, planting a blade, stops abruptly. The two girls embrace and then, holding both hands, turn slowly around each other as they talk excitedly. White vapor spills from their mouths. From his bench Roman catches the melodious laughter of the girl in red. The two girls, who have obviously agreed on something, kiss lightly on the lips. Rosalyn skates over to the edge of the pond near Roman's bench. "You'll never guess who I met!" she says excitedly. "It's my cousin Yulia Naumovna. Her father tried to park her in a Swiss boarding school, but she managed to get herself expelled—typical Yulia, she was caught posing nude for a hot Italian painter, which is what we were laughing about. Did you see her skate? When she was sweet sixteen, there was some talk of her turning professional. Her parents nicknamed her Scapegrace because she has a talent for mischief. Oh my God, when we were kids, she was forever in hot water for something she did or something she should have done and didn't. She's invited me to her birthday party. It begins at eleven tonight—she turns twenty-two at the stroke of twelve. Her father has rented out the entire dining room of the Metropol. When I said I was with a friend, she told me to bring you along."

"Who is this father of hers that rents the dining room at the Metropol?" Roman asks.

Mika materializes behind Roman's bench. "Her father is Naum Caplan," he announces in a hard voice. "No question of your going to a party hosted by the Caplan clan." He leans down and murmurs in Roman's ear. "They are the Jew *vory* who are aching for a *razborka* with your father."

"Come on, Roman, you're not going to let your gorilla spoil our fun."

"It's okay, Mika. I've been away for three months. Nobody will recognize me without my beard."

"I'm your father's brigadier, and I am telling you not to go to this Caplan party."

Roman eyes his bodyguard. "My father drummed into me that the more we fear to do things, the more we need to do them."

Rosalyn agrees. "The Tibetan Buddhists call it *chöd*—embrace the thing you fear."

Mika is not pleased. "How the hell will I explain this to your father?"

"If the subject comes up, which it won't if you don't raise it, tell him I decided to infiltrate the enemy."

Mika drives them back to Rosalyn's flat so she can change into something more appropriate for a midnight party at the Metropol, which turns out to be a body-hugging knee-length dress with a plunging neckline that leaves little to the imagination. When they come downstairs ten minutes later, Mika has disappeared. Roman shrugs. Using the pay phone in the lobby, he calls a taxi service. Twenty minutes later the two of them arrive at the hotel across from the Bolshoi. In the lobby, waiters are pushing carts filled with bottles of champagne toward the dining room. "Here goes nothing," Roman mutters as they check their coats and fall in behind one of the carts.

Guards are inspecting invitations and body searching guests at the doorway of the great dining hall with its vast stained-glass skylight. "I'm Yulia Caplan's cousin," Rosalyn tells one of them who stops her with a palm on her chest. "She invited me. Us. Ask her if you don't believe me." The guard takes in her plunging neckline and waves her past. "He's with me," Rosalyn calls over her shoulder.

"Are you carrying?" the guard asks Roman.

"I'm carrying the weight of the world on my shoulders," Roman says.

"Very funny." The guard pats him down from his armpits to his ankles, then jerks his head for him to follow Rosalyn. Inside, the tables have been pushed to the sides and dozens of young couples are dancing to American rock and roll blaring from loudspeakers. Rosalyn spots her cousin near the stage and plowing through the crush of guests, pulling Roman along behind her, she crosses the dining hall. "Happy twenty-two, Yulia," she cries as the girls hug. "Say hello to my friend. His name is Roman."

Yulia, wearing the short fiery-red skirt from the ice rink but without the tights, and a man's pleated tuxedo shirt with the cuffs rolled up to her elbows, turns to Roman. He can't help noticing that her lips are painted the same color as her skirt. Except for a single braid laced with red wool falling over one ear, her long dark hair caresses her shoulders. "So: Hello to Rosalyn's friend."

Roman glances around the great hall. "Hell of a way to celebrate a birthday."

"It was my father's idea. His motto in life is, 'If you're going hog, you might as well go whole hog.' Which, when you think about it, is pretty hilarious coming from an Israelite who refuses to eat pork."

There is a scratchy sound as someone lifts the needle off the rock and roll record. The great Kremlin clock can be heard tolling the midnight hour. At the last stroke of twelve, the four-man band on the stage fills the dining hall with a fanfare. A thin young man in a three-piece Italian suit hikes himself onto the stage, raises the microphone to the level of his lips. "I happen to be the birthday girl's kid cousin, Tzuf," he announces, leaning over the microphone, his voice pealing from the loudspeakers. The microphone squeals. Tzuf taps it with a fingernail. "We are almost twins, so to speak, but she was born twelve minutes before me and never lets me forget it. My prematurely thinning hair notwithstanding, she claims that as she has been around twelve minutes longer, she is more mature than me and better armed to skirt life's booby traps. More mature, maybe. Better armed?" Tzuf produces a pistol from an ankle holster. "I don't think so." He lets the laughter subside. "But from someone who has the same birthday as you, Yulia, happy birthday to the both of us. Long life, short loves, but many of them!"

The couples in the hall applaud wildly. The older men sitting at tables, many of them with younger women, stamp their feet. Naum Caplan, a rail-thin man with a tuft of white hair under his lower lip and a mane of white hair falling to the crimson turtle-neck of his sweater, steps up to the microphone to welcome his guests. "For those of you who are not of the Israelite persuasion, let me explain a few basics," he begins. "My father, may he rest in whatever peace can be found in the shadow of the valley of Gehenna, was agnostic, but he kept kosher in case it turned out there was a God. He had me circumcised for the same reason. Keeping kosher, circumcising your male children, is a way of hedging your bets, he would say. I also hedge my bets—I am careful not to kill anyone on the Sabbath in case it turns out there is a God." Caplan, who is legendary in *vory* circles for having cornered the Russian market in imported computers after the mysterious deaths of his competitors, lets the awkward laughter subside. "There is a biblical explanation for why I am careful not to kill anyone on the Sabbath," he goes on. "Our rabbis tell us that our sages tell us that the Torah tells us that if you don't keep the Sabbath, you are violating all six hundred thirteen of its sacred commandments. And the penalty for violating even one commandment is death. Which is why I say to my Jewish friends—also to my friends who belong to the Jewish sect Christianity—who have surely managed to violate at least one of God's six hundred thirteen commandments today: You are going to get yourselves murdered, but trust me, if it's on the Sabbath you can bet it will not be by me. As for the six other days of the week . . ." Smiling innocently, Caplan lets the thought hang in the air.

Everyone laughs, though Roman notices some laugh less than others.

"My father could have been a stand-up comic instead of a businessman," Yulia declares.

"There are people here who don't think he is funny," Roman says, but his words are lost in the applause.

In the dining hall, the music starts up again. Yulia's cousin Tzuf pulls his sister, Rosalyn, onto the dance floor. Yulia sinks into a chair next to Roman, her long legs stretched out in front of her.

Roman tries to strike up a conversation. "Rosalyn tells me you spent time in Switzerland."

"I did. The climate didn't agree with me—it wasn't cold enough."

"You must love Moscow on days like this."

"I adore Moscow every day of the year, but especially in the winter, when I can go skating. How about you? Do you love Moscow?"

"I'm not sure yet. I've been off in London for several months. The climate there didn't agree with me either. I'm not talking weather, I'm talking about their MI5 people treating every Russian like a Corsican mafioso."

Yulia laughs that melodious laugh he first heard floating across the skating pond. "Aren't they Corsican mafiosi?"

"Some are, some aren't." Roman glances at her. "What did your father give you for your birthday?"

"My dream car—a baby-blue Porsche 911 Turbo three-point-three-liter flat six. I had a Mercedes 190 SL in Switzerland that had the rotten luck to run into a tree. It was, it goes without saying, the tree's fault." Again the melodious laughter. "In Switzerland, they don't beat about the bush—when a car hits a tree, they decapitate the tree."

"Which is why those winding, picturesque roads are no longer lined with trees."

"Which is why," she agrees.

Roman hesitates. "Listen, I can get two tickets for the opening night of Prokofiev's *Romeo and Juliet* tomorrow." He looks at his watch. "Or should I say today. Maïa Plissetskaïa is dancing Juliet."

"Nobody in Moscow, with the possible exception of Comrade Yeltsin, can get two tickets to opening night of Plissetskaïa's Juliet."

"If I get Yeltsin's tickets, will you come with me?"

She turns to look at him with glacial coldness. "No."

"No?"

"Who are you that you don't understand the word *no*?"

"I've been told I'm someone from another planet. If you change your mind—"

She blurts out in a hoarse whisper, "Why are you doing this to me? Why are you doing this to yourself?"

"I had a wild idea you could save me from the cloud I've been flying in."

"You speak in riddles. I've got this right, right? You *are* my cousin Rosalyn's boyfriend?"

"Would it change things if I were her *ex*-boyfriend?"

"Fuck you, Roman from another planet."

"Fuck me," he agrees.

"What do you really want?"

"To make a good first impression on you."

"You only get one chance to make a first impression. You blew it."

"I'll be waiting outside the Bolshoi at seven thirty. If you don't turn up, I'll give the tickets to the oldest and ugliest woman queuing in the hope of getting to see Plissetskaïa dance Juliet."

"I would not want to deprive the oldest and ugliest woman of seeing Plissetskaïa dance Juliet." Yulia bounds from her chair so quickly it falls over backward. Heads turn.

Rosalyn comes over. "What the hell did you say to make her angry, Roman?"

"I told her I was from another planet. I think she believed me and it frightened her off."

Stamping his feet in the snow to keep blood circulating in his toes, Roman glances at his Patek Philippe. It is twelve minutes past seven thirty and eighteen minutes to curtain call, and according to the wristwatch, a new moon is just below the horizon. He waits another three minutes, scanning the crowd from the steps of the Bolshoi, hoping against hope she will turn up, and a bit startled at the seed of hope that Yulia has planted in him. At fifteen to the hour, he gives up. There are a dozen people scattered around the entrance eager to come across someone with a ticket too many. On the sidewalk, off to one side, Roman spots an ancient woman shivering in a cloth coat, her head covered in an army cap with the earflaps down. He plants himself in front of her. "Looking for a ticket to *Romeo and Juliet*?"

The woman lifts the flap off one ear. "What say?"

Roman holds out the tickets. "Here are two—you can sell one for a small fortune and use the other. They're first-row balcony."

The woman, with tears brimming in her eyes, takes the tickets and begins to fumble with a small purse. "How much—"

"I'm not selling them to you. I am giving them to you."

The woman clicks open her purse and pulls out a fistful of ruble notes. But Roman is already walking rapidly away. Calling out "*Gospodin! Gospodin!*" the woman stumbles after him, but Roman breaks into a trot. The woman, waving the rubles in her hand, abandons the chase and, barely believing her good fortune, turns back toward the Bolshoi.

6
RASPUTIN: YO, TZUF, HERE WE ARE . . .

MOSCOW

A crumb of backstory

before picking up the frontstory

There are two things that never fail to piss me off. The first is when someone does not believe me when I tell them I am the grandson of the murdered holy monk Grigori Efimovich Rasputin, who, when he roamed across the parched steppes of Siberia to the Winter Palace of Tsar Nicholas, was saluted by the long wooden arms of water wells bowing as he passed, so it was said. And so one of his daughters, my mother, claimed to have seen with her own eyes. The second is when someone accepts that I am the grandson of the infamous *strannik*, the wanderer, who hung out in the plush Hotel de Europe in Petrograd surrounded by royal ladies-in-waiting wearing low-cut dresses (his daughter, my mother, heard this from the lips of the duchess of something or other) but doesn't give a flying fuck. Obviously, the promised land for my martyred grandfather was the bedchamber, more often than not inhabited by the chosen female who sucked him into her womb and welcomed his seed as if it were a gift from God, which explains how the far-from-celibate monk came to sire three girls and three sons. One of the three girls turned out to be my mother, Maria Rasputina. She was born in 1898 and wound up as something of a wanderer herself, fleeing one jump ahead of the Bolsheviks to Rumania, then to France, then to Germany, eventually winding up, of all places, in the United States of North America, where she met her Maker in 1977. As for me, I was born in 1945, when Maria was an overripe forty-seven. To answer your question before you ask it, I don't recall her talking much about her father—given his disrepute (rumors circulated that he was fucking the tsar's tsarina, though personally I think he was too smart to have taken the risk), the subject was for the most part taboo. I do remember her remembering him saying something about man being created in the image of God the Father and Jesus Christ the Son. (I suppose he wasn't sure what the Holy Ghost looked like, which explains why he left him out of the Trinity.) Thus, man, created in the image of God the Father, is sacred. And if man is sacred, his bodily excretions are likewise sacred, so my grandfather apparently reasoned. Which is why, when he masturbated, which folklore has it was five or six times a day, he ejaculated into the palm of his hand and sprinkled the sacred seed like holy water on the ankles of the tsar's kid Alexei to soothe the agony in his joints caused by incurable hemophilia. I myself, like the *strannik* Rasputin, am not an educated man. On one of his thousand-kilometer walks, Grandfather Grigori was said to have come across a hermit monk who could read Latin. This monk would quote from an ode written two decades before the birth of our Savior by someone name of Horace: *Carpe diem, quam minimum credula postero*, which I understand to mean something along the lines of *Pluck the day as you would a ripe apple that is begging to be eaten, but for Christ's sake don't hold out hope for tomorrow.*

If an uneducated man can be said to have a worldview, this more or less sums up mine.

Which brings me to the here and now in this saga Littell is telling, the details of which are fixed in my brain because of what transpired next. So: Always on the lookout for ripe apples, I would jot down the names of the Ossetes queuing in the first-floor antechamber of the tsarist banker's mansion, one name to a file card, and note what favor they were hoping to get from my *pakhan*, Timur. On this particular winter morning—I remember it was a Saturday—there were twin brothers, Pavel and Pyotr, who were angling for good-paying jobs in a factory importing denim and producing blue jeans with French labels. There was a woman named Galina hoping to get her son, who had lost a leg in Afghanistan, a West German prosthesis to replace his Russian limb from the Great Patriotic War that didn't bend at the knee. And there was Tamara, the young and not unattractive widow of an Ossete brigadier gunned down in the early days of the Great Moscow Turf War. She received a monthly stipend from Timur but was asking for a raise because her landlord had doubled the rent.

With the file cards in hand, I made my way as usual to the third floor, where Timur was holding his weekly council of brigadiers. Nine of our guys were sitting around a long table. Roman, watching from a seat along one wall, nodded at me as I handed Timur the file cards and took my place at the table immediately to his right, befitting my rank of chief brigadier. Two of our veteran *vory* enforcers, Lice and Spare Rib, and the keeper of the Ossete common fund, the Greek, had hiked themselves onto windowsills and looked on. The Ossetes' newest sixer, a twenty-four-year-old we'd nicknamed the Argentine when he came on board (Ossete on his father's side, Argentine on his mother's side, he'd made the mistake of visiting his mother's mother in Buenos Aires when he was thirteen and gotten pressed into the Argentine army for six years), stood with his back against the door of Timur's inner sanctum. The *pakhan*, wearing a gray woolen Ossete mountain robe over his suit jacket, with the curved dagger I'd given him for his seventieth birthday tucked into the belt, presided from the head of the table. I recollect a brigadier name of Shota speaking up as I settled into my seat. "I propose we provide a roof to a chain of ice cream shops in Moscow called Baskin-Robbins. They currently pay three hundred US a month to the Khozyain *pakhan* Bob Efimoviff, but as he is doing time in the *zona*—he has fourteen months left on a three-year sentence for tax evasion—I figure the Baskin-Robbins people are ripe for a new arrangement."

As was his habit, Timur shut his eyes and pondered Shota's pitch before finally shaking his head. "Removing an existing roof involves certain risks, even a small war with the Khozyain *vory*," is what I remember him saying. "Besides which, it is against our *vory* code to seize an asset from someone serving a sentence in the *zona*. We will revisit the question when Bob Efimoviff gets out of prison. If we feel the Baskin-Robbins roof fits our portfolio, we can negotiate some kind of trade-off. I know Bob personally. He is a reasonable man who will respond reasonably so long as he is respected and our *vory* code governs the negotiation. What else?"

A bearded brigadier named Ruslan hiked a hand. "A West German fashion model name of"—he glanced at a paper—"Schiffer, Claudia, who is said to resemble the French film star Brigitte Bardot, is thinking of visiting Moscow. A friend of a friend of her agent has sounded us out about providing bodyguards."

"Pity Brigitte Bardot is not thinking of visiting Moscow,"

the Greek quipped from the windowsill. The brigadiers around the table laughed between their teeth. I likewise was unable to suppress a smile.

Timur, who abandoned the stock of smiles we are all born with back in Strict Regime Corrective Labor Colony No. 40, did not crack a smile. "I can't see how we would be stepping on anyone's toes if we agree to this. Tell the friend of a friend that we are open to an arrangement. We charge the standard fee—one hundred US per bodyguard, six bodyguards per shift, three shifts every twenty-four hours, plus a hundred a day to rent the bulletproof limousine for the principal and fifty a day for the backup car." He looked around. "Anything else?"

A young brigadier named Soslan, who had been an enforcer the last time Roman sat in on one of Timur's conclaves, spoke up. "I think there is a killing to be made escorting trucks filled with West European merchandise through the Ukraine to Moscow."

"*Pakhan*, the Chechen *vory* control that route," the Greek reminded Timur.

Soslan stuck to his guns. I remember him saying something along the lines of "The word on the street is the Chechens are incapable of providing sufficient protection. The route has become so dangerous—three or four trucks are hijacked every day under the Chechens' noses—the trucking companies are having trouble recruiting drivers even when they offer bonuses. Given our reputation—given *your* reputation, *pakhan*—I believe we could get a piece of this action without stepping on Chechen toes."

Timur, his brow crinkling into freshly plowed furrows, glanced over at me. "What does our chief brigadier think, Mika?"

My luck, I'd looked into the situation in the Ukraine the week before when I heard a reporter on television describe the hijacking going on there. "If you ask me, *pakhan*, providing protection to trucks crossing the Ukraine—even if they are organized in convoys—would stretch our resources too thin. We need to concentrate on our home turf. Let one of those new private protection companies—Baltik Escort, for instance, which has been recruiting enforcers from police units in Leningrad—handle the contract on condition they agree to keep out of our hair when the trucks reach Moscow."

I will not conceal the surge of satisfaction I felt when I heard Timur declare, "I agree with Mika. The more pressing problem will be to keep the Jews out of our hair here in Moscow. They have their eye on our *krysha* contract with Smirnoff Vodka. Last weekend their thugs attacked the sixers we posted at the Smirnoff distillery. Our people were forced to lie facedown in the snow for two hours before I got the Jew *pakhan* Naum Caplan on the phone and read him the riot act. I told him, 'We don't want to start a war with you'—Mika says my broken nostril whistled as I spoke in the glacial tone I use when I am trying to control my temper—'but if one starts, you can be sure we will not lose it.'"

I couldn't resist picking up the story. "The *pakhan* held the phone away from his ear so I could monitor the conversation," I explained. "I could hear Caplan swearing it was all a misunderstanding, that he wasn't looking for a *razborka*. One hell of a misunderstanding!"

"I told him to call off his thugs or a shootout would come looking for him," Timur recounted with a snicker. "Our boys were released within minutes."

Timur looked around the table. "Well, if there is nothing else," he said, scraping back his chair and getting to his feet.

Taking his cue from the *pakhan*, Lice began to hand out small kitchen tumblers filled with fermented Ossetian arak while Spare Rib passed around mint chocolates that Timur, famous for his sweet tooth even in the *zona*, got delivered weekly by an English start-up in Moscow named, aptly, Sweet Tooth Ltd. Nibbling on a mint, Timur raised his glass and offered up his usual toast. "To our *vory v zakone*, may we never forget where we come from, the better to get where we're going."

"*Uraa*, esteemed Timur," I cried, holding my glass high to salute the *pakhan*.

"*Uraaa*, Timur the Lame!" the brigadiers shouted in chorus, and clanking glasses, we all threw back our heads and downed the arak.

Lice was refilling the tumblers, as I reconstruct the scene, when the red telephone on a sideboard started ringing. The brigadiers stopped drinking and looked at Timur, who stared at the phone as the shrill sound filled the room, then nodded at me. I went over to answer it. Knowing me, I suspect my eyes would have narrowed into a squint as I held the phone to my ear, listening intently. "Okay," I remember snapping into the mouthpiece. "Keep them talking. We'll be there in twenty minutes."

"What is it?" Timur wanted to know.

"Caplan's nephew, along with some of his thugs, turned up at that new Porsche dealer, Car Maintenance Station Number Seven," I explained. "The Jews didn't believe them when they said they already had a roof. Caplan's people are trying to pass it off as a *probivka*"—only probing!—"but the Porsche manager is afraid it won't take much to turn it into a *naezd*"—an assault. As Timur's senior brigadier, I knew the drill. There was no time to waste. I waved to Lice and Spare Rib and the Argentine to follow me.

Timur grabbed my elbow and I heard him say, very quietly, "Take Roman with you—he needs to get his feet wet."

Speeding through Moscow in my Range Rover, I ran a dozen red lights and three intersections with uniformed militiamen frantically blowing whistles when I didn't slow down. Spotting

Roman's grimace, I couldn't contain a laugh. "Think Italy," I told him, "where stoplights and cops wildly waving batons are merely a suggestion." The Argentine, in the back seat with Lice and Spare Rib, kept igniting his Zippo lighter and then smothering the flame with the lid. I eyed him in the rearview mirror. "Do me a favor and knock that off, huh?" I growled from the driver's seat. "You are making us all nervous."

Lice leaned forward. "Do we need artillery, Mika?" he asked.

"Yes, we need artillery; it depends on Caplan's people whether we use it or not," I told him. Opening the backseat armrest, Lice took out three semiautomatic Walther P38s and two 9mm Belgium Parabellums fitted with silencers and passed them around. I saw Roman take off his gloves and, punching a magazine into a P38, chamber a round. "If it turns into a *naezd*," I instructed the enforcers in the back seat, "the Parabellums shoot first. Less noise that way."

I eased the Range Rover into the alley behind Car Maintenance Station No. 7 and cut the motor. The five of us, each holding a pistol along the seam of his trousers, made our way down the alley to the garage's workshop. A Toyota Hilux pickup was parked in the alley alongside the overhead double door, which was half-raised. I ducked and stole a quick look inside, then held up the five fingers of my left hand. "Five of them," Roman told the others under his breath.

Angry voices could be heard coming from the workshop. "How many times do I have to tell you we already got a roof—"

"The top Porsche dealer in Moscow could use a new roof that doesn't leak."

"You need to talk to the *pakhan* Timur and his Ossete *vory*, not us."

"We are starting with you. We will deal with the *pakhan* Timur and his Ossete *vory* when the time comes."

Roman and I ducked under the half-raised garage door, our three enforcers right behind us. The five of us spread out inside, our pistols visible in our fists. The garage manager in a business suit and two mechanics in overalls spotted us first and, anticipating a shootout, backed away. The five Caplan *vory*, four of them dressed in the dumb baggy trousers Caplan's enforcers sported, each with a shotgun slung over a shoulder on a gaudy cloth strap, were standing near a four-post lift with a Porsche convertible up on it. Seeing the manager backing away, they turned to face us.

"Yo, Tzuf, if you're planning to deal with Timur and his Ossete *vory*," I announced with a dry laugh, "you have lucked out. Here we are."

Tzuf's pale face creased into a nervous smile. "Why the pistols?" he asked with mock innocence, his hands spread wide. "Hey, Rasputin, we only stopped by to sound out the situation. We are asking for a *vory* conference to allocate territory. Car Maintenance Station Number Seven opened for business three weeks ago. The last *strelka* did not assign the roof here to Timur's Ossetes."

I grinned at Tzuf. "The last *strelka* assigned this *neighborhood* to Timur's Ossetes," I remember saying. "There is nothing to talk about here. You boys do not want to leave your Toyota outside too long. It is illegal to park in the alley. A cop might come along and give you a ticket."

Never taking his eyes off me, Tzuf backed toward the garage door. My guys pulled back on either side as the Jews filed past. The Argentine must have noticed one of the enforcers starting to slip a hand into a pants pocket because he said, very quietly, "You do not want to go there unless you need another buttonhole in the pocket flap." Tzuf's enforcer, his hand on the grip of the pistol that was surely in his pocket, hesitated. For an instant it could have gone either way. Then I saw the Argentine, his hand a blur of motion, bring up one of the Parabellums fitted with a silencer and shoot from the hip. We all heard the soft spit of air as the blunt Browning Long bullet shattered the enforcer's kneecap. He shrieked in pain and fell back into the arms of the other enforcers. "You will need to get him to a clinic real fast if you want to save the leg," the Argentine said with an edgy giggle.

Tzuf and his men carried the moaning enforcer to their Toyota. "This is not going away!" Tzuf yelled as they lifted the wounded enforcer into the back of the pickup. The car's motor sputtered to life and the Toyota, with pebbles crunching under its wheels, crawled toward the far end of the alley.

"What do we do if they pay us another visit?" the garage manager asked.

I reassured him. "Our *pakhan* will put in a friendly call to the Israelite *pakhan* Caplan. You will not be seeing these jokers again. Take my word for it."

Backing the Range Rover out of the alley, I headed toward the boulevard. "You made a big mistake shooting the Jew," I told the Argentine, looking at him in the rearview mirror.

"I could tell he had his paw on a pistol, Mika," the Argentine, subdued, muttered. I could hear him sniffling as if he had caught a cold. "If there was shooting," he went on plaintively, "you said for the Parabellums to shoot first."

"Whichever," I said. "Timur will not be thrilled."

As the Range Rover reached the corner, Roman noticed a baby-blue Porsche 911 pulling up to the glass front door of the garage. The driver—a woman, judging from the profile—began honking her horn impatiently. I noticed Roman noticing. "You recognize the driver?" I asked him.

"I recognize the car," he said. He opened the passenger door and called back through the window, "Don't wait for me."

Shrugging, I threw the car into gear and edged into the boulevard traffic. I had too much on my mind—for starters, explaining to the *pakhan* why the Argentine had shot one of the Jews in the knee—to worry about Roman trying to pick up a girl driving a Porsche.

7
ROMAN: HOPING FOR A SECOND CHANCE TO MAKE A GOOD FIRST IMPRESSION . . .

MOSCOW

More frontstory

Roman walks around to the driver's window of the Porsche and motions for the woman to lower it. "We meet again," he announces.

"Unfortunately. Did you give the Bolshoi tickets to the oldest and ugliest woman queuing for *Romeo and Juliet*?"

"I did. She chased after me waving a fistful of rubles, but as I was fifty years younger I managed to outrun her. What are you doing here with your new birthday toy?"

"Not that it's any of your business, but this happens to be the dealership that sold the Porsche to my father. When they delivered it they neglected to supply the code for the radio. They promised to give it to me if I turned up. So up I turned. But nobody seems to want to open the front door."

Roman gestures for her to move over. Yulia, lost in a double-breasted midnight-blue naval officer's greatcoat, tilts her head quizzically and regards him for a long moment, then with an exasperated toss of a shoulder slides over onto the passenger seat. Roman climbs in behind the wheel, throws the car into reverse, and backs into the boulevard, then, shifting through the gears, heads into town. Casting nervous glances at Roman, Yulia demands, "Where are you taking me in *my* car?"

"To visit a grave."

Unlike Mika, Roman stops at the red lights and at intersections until the militiaman waves him through. He pulls up in front of the Novodevichy Cemetery, cuts the motor, and leads Yulia into the cemetery and onto the path going off to the right. "Here it is," he says, sidling through a waist-high hedge to stand in front of the white stele of a young woman, her right hand resting protectively on her marble throat. Someone had draped the woman's marble head with a garland of red roses that had long since wilted.

"I've meandered through this cemetery a dozen times but I never saw this tomb," Yulia murmurs. "Who was she?"

"Stalin's second wife, Nadezhda Alliluyeva-Stalina." The air is glacial. Vapor escapes from Roman's mouth as he talks. "On the ninth of November 1932, at the tender age of thirty-one, she killed herself with a pistol her brother brought back to her from Germany."

"Why are you showing me this?"

"I'm hoping for a second chance to make a good first impression." Roman retrieves a wilted rose that has fallen to the ground and puts it back on Nadezhda's marble forehead. "There was a Stalin before his wife committed suicide and a Stalin after she shot herself, which meant there was a Russia before November 1932 and a Russia afterward. Kirov was murdered *after* Nadezhda's suicide. Stalin killed off all the old Bolsheviks—Zinoviev, Kamenev, Bukharin, Rykov, Trotsky—*after* Nadezhda's suicide. He murdered thousands of the Red Army's senior officers, including Marshal Tukhachevsky, *after* Nadezhda's suicide."

"I hate to admit it, but your first impression is better the second time around. Don't let the compliment go to your head—you had nowhere to go but up. Where did you learn so much about Russian history?"

"In London I read books that are not published here. Yet." He runs a thumb over the name *Stalina* scored into the stele. "Hundreds of books have been written about Stalin, trying to figure out what made him tick—what part paranoid peasant, what part ruthless dictator, what part Marxist idealist, what part Leninist pragmatist, what part Georgian *vin ordinaire* bottled in Moscow. Nadezhda's tomb tells you more about Stalin than all the biographies. This beautiful woman, the mother of two of his children, preferred to kill herself than to sleep with him again." Embarrassed by the seriousness of the conversation, Roman coughs up a mirthless laugh. "On the off chance you don't have other plans, a friend told me about a new restaurant across the street from here. He said their speciality is grilled flatbreads stuffed with lamb." There is a mischievous glint in his eyes as he adds, "The restaurant is Georgian, so don't expect the food to be kosher."

A flicker of a half-smile materializes on Yulia's lips. "I also eat nonkosher."

"Is that a yes?"

"At my birthday party you didn't understand the word *no*. Now you don't understand the word *yes*."

"I'm better with *yes* than *no*," Roman tells her. He takes hold of Yulia's elbow. She doesn't pull away.

The Georgian restaurant, on the ground floor of a once-grand town house, is crowded with noisy American tourists who drink wine as if it were water and laugh loudly. Slipping the headwaiter fifty rubles, Roman snares a corner table in the back of the restaurant near the swinging doors to the kitchen. Yulia hangs her naval greatcoat on a peg embedded in the wall, arranges the pleats of her ankle-length polka-dot dress as she settles onto her seat. When a bottle of Saint Emilion is uncorked, Roman waves the waiter away and fills the two wineglasses himself. "To us," he says, raising his glass.

"There is a you and there is a me," Yulia corrects him. "There is no us, Roman."

"Yet."

"Listen, Roman from another planet, I know which planet you come from. My cousin Rosalyn told me. You remember Rosalyn, don't you? You are the son of the Ossete *pakhan* they call Timur the Lame. I am the daughter of the Israelite *pakhan* Naum Caplan. If my father found me with you . . ."

What she leaves unsaid hangs in the air between them. Roman prods her. "What would he do?"

Yulia turns away.

"What would he do?" he insists.

She turns back and looks him unblinkingly in the eye. "He would kill you."

"Unless it was the Sabbath," he jokes.

"On the Sabbath, he would make an exception for the son of Timur the Lame."

"Having a meal with me in a restaurant has to be an adventure for a Swiss-finishing-school girl like you."

"I'm not looking for adventure, Roman."

He sips his wine. "You're looking for what, then?"

"I have frightening nightmares: Every time I say goodbye to my father, to my uncle Mordechai, to my cousin Tzuf, I think, *Oh my God, it could be the last time I see them alive.* Especially Tzuf—he is really crazy wild, always looking for trouble when trouble isn't looking for him. What I need, Roman, is something an Ossete *vory* can't give me—a refuge, a haven, a safe harbor where . . ." Yulia blinks away the trace of emotion. "Where viciousness haunts only your sleep, not your waking hours."

"Consider the possibility—consider the *probability*—that viciousness is written into our genes," Roman says. "In the Middle Ages, the ancestors of my London friend Anthony organized very public executions. The condemned man was dragged to the scaffold and hanged until he was almost dead, then, while he was still alive, his intestines were cut out. After which his body was sawed into four parts. The executed man was said to have been drawn and quartered. Talk about viciousness!"

"Our Russian *vory* aren't far behind your medieval Brits," Yulia says. "Late last month the Azerbaijani kidnapped two of my father's *vory*. I knew one of them. His name was David; he used to chauffeur me around Moscow before I got my driver's license. The Azerbaijani sent a message telling my father he could find the two *vory* in a deserted hangar near the airport."

"And did he? Find his *vory* in the hangar?"

"He found their bodies. He never did find their heads."

Roman refills Yulia's wineglass. After a while he says, "What did the *pakhan* Caplan do when he found the decapitated bodies?"

"My father doesn't believe in the Bible, but he does believe in the biblical injunction *an eye for an eye*. What he did turned up as a small item on a back page of *Pravda* under the headline *Three Azerbaijani killed in explosion*." Yulia dips a forefinger into the wineglass and carefully moistens her lips with a fingertip as if she's applying lipstick. "Don't you see it, Roman? We are particles of dust, trapped in a vicious circle that goes by the name of Russia, meekly waiting our turn to be swept up and thrown into the bin."

"Dust to dust," he murmurs.

"Ashes to ashes," she says with a snicker that has the faintest suggestion of a sob in it.

"There has to be a way out," Roman says after a moment, trying to convince himself more than her.

"There is no way out until you can cry over spilt milk."

He glances quickly at her. "Want to tell me about your spilt milk?"

She shakes her head vigorously. "No. Absolutely not." She takes a deep breath. "Not yet."

Later, over dessert, Roman works up the nerve to blurt out, "We can't stop here, Yulia. I need to see you again."

"Is that smart?"

"It's a matter of life or death for me," he says intently.

"It could be a matter of life or death for you, Roman."

"I'll risk that." He is embarrassed by what he is going to say but that doesn't stop him from saying it. "Hey, will you fuck with me, Yulia?"

"Will once quench your thirst?"

"Once can lead to twice. And twice can end up . . . who knows where."

Outside the restaurant, Yulia, pulling up the collar of her navy greatcoat, sucks the arctic air into her lungs. "Here's the thing: I'm going to a wedding in the Bolshaya Bronnaya Synagogue on Saturday. In Stalin's time the rabbi was executed and the synagogue was turned into a trade union hall, but the Jewish community is restoring it. My girlfriend's wedding will be the first Jewish ceremony there since the Bolshevik Revolution. It ought to be over by five. There will be so many guests nobody will notice if I skip the party afterward. I'll park the Porsche behind the synagogue and leave the key under the right front wheel."

Roman moves closer to her but she puts the palm of her hand on his chest. "This is insane," she whispers.

"Insane is when you play chess against yourself," Roman says. He shakes his head, bites his lip. "Insane is when you turn back before you know where the road goes."

8
OSIP AXELROD: SO LONG AS THE VIOLENCE APPEARS RANDOM—A CORPSE HERE, A CORPSE THERE . . .

MOSCOW

Wednesday, January 8, 1992

Osip Axelrod, at thirty-three a rising star in intelligence circles, recently named chief of the Sixth Bureau of the Organized Crime Control Department, flicks the button on his intercom. "Male or female?" he demands.

"This is your name day, Chief. Female," his trainee, Misha, reports.

"What's she look like?"

"Pushing forty from the wrong side, good looking if you need glasses and can't remember where you put them. Blond, maybe bleached, maybe not—I'm too young to be an expert on female hair. Leather jeans tucked into boots, tight ribbed black sweater."

"Brassiere?"

"Couldn't tell. Her coat was unbuttoned but she was still wearing it."

"Wedding band?"

"Gloves."

"Okay, send her in."

Osip's four thirty is ushered into the office. "Adelgunde Möller, *Berliner Zeitung*," she says in English, hanging her coat on the back of the door. "Sorry I don't speak Russian," she adds, removing her gloves and offering to shake hands.

Osip spots a gold wedding band on the fourth finger of her left hand. "I'm not sorry I don't speak German," he remarks, ignoring her outstretched hand, motioning her to the seat across from the kitchen table that serves as a desk. "Both my mother and her parents lived in the village of Kalach, on the Don near Stalingrad. One day—it was late January 1942, so sun drenched the temperature rose to minus thirty—they along with hundreds of other Jews were herded onto the frozen river and shot. To save ammunition the Wehrmacht lined them up one behind the other so that each bullet would kill four or five Jews, then used a flame-thrower to melt the ice so the bodies would vanish into the Don."

"If you're trying to blame me for war crimes committed before I was born, you must believe in collective guilt. If you believe in collective guilt, you would be responsible for the millions Stalin murdered."

"Actually, I do think Russians—me included, though I was born five years after Stalin died—must take responsibility for Stalin's crimes. It was Russian police who arrested people; it was Russian judges who sentenced them to execution or prison; it was Russian guards who ran the camps in what Solzhenitsyn called the Gulag Archipelago. But all that's another story. I was simply telling you why I don't regret not speaking German."

"Perhaps we should start over. Thank you for according me the interview—"

"I scheduled the interview because my director, who runs the MVD's Organized Crime Control Department, instructed me to. You wouldn't know how to work this coffee machine? It's East German. I'm not sure if it's broken or I just don't understand the instructions, which, logically enough, are in German."

"I'm not a coffee-machine repairman, Mr. Axelrod. I'm the Moscow correspondent of the *Berliner Zeitung*. Can we begin?"

Osip shoves a pile of dossiers on the table to one side. "Begin, begin. I am all ears," he announces, scratching absently at one of them with a fingernail.

Frau Möller turns on a small Sony cassette recorder with the built-in microphone aimed at Osip. "Your Organized Crime Control Department has been criticized for attacking the problem of organized crime half-heartedly—"

Osip flips the button on the intercom. "Misha, is your coffee machine working?"

"Affirmative."

"Two American coffees." He looks up. "Cream? Sugar?"

Adelgunde Möller takes a deep breath to swallow her exasperation. "No cream. One lump of sugar."

"No cream. Put some sugar on a dish. Don't forget spoons." Osip loosens the knot of his tie and talks directly into Frau Möller's cassette contraption. "'Attacking crime half-heartedly.' Half-heartedness would have the advantage of being in character, considering the building we're in."

"I'm not sure I—"

"This eyesore of a building is a perfect symbol of the seventy-year Soviet plague. When the Ministry of Internal Affairs—what you call the MVD—was created after the Great Patriotic War, the original plan was for it to be housed in a showcase twenty-story building. Fortunately, from an aesthetic point of view, they ran out of money and material at the tenth floor. At which point some genius had the brilliant idea of putting a roof on the half-built building—a real roof, the kind that keeps out rain, not the 'roof' provided by our *vory v zakone* these days—and announcing it was finished." Osip snickers. "Fact is, under the Soviet glaze the USSR was a third-world piece of crockery."

"You refer to the seventy-year Soviet plague, Mr. Axelrod. Were you anti-Soviet *during* the Soviet plague?"

It dawns on Osip that he is talking to a real journalist, not a Soviet journalist. "When Nikita Khrushchev denounced Stalin's crimes at the Twentieth Party Congress—that was in 1956, three years after Stalin's death—the story goes that someone passed a note up to him on the podium. He read it aloud to the delegates at the Congress: *Where were you when Stalin was committing these crimes?* the note demanded. Khrushchev waved the scrap of paper angrily. 'Who wrote this? Who wrote this?' he shouted. Naturally, nobody stood up and identified himself as the author. At which point Khrushchev is supposed to have bellowed, 'That's where I was!'"

"You're telling me that that's where you were too during what you now call the Soviet plague?"

"Which is why I bear a responsibility for Stalin's crimes." Toying with the bayonet he uses to open letters, Osip studies the journalist across the kitchen table. "I'll take a wild guess: That's where your father and grandfather were, along with the other seventy million Germans, during the Hitler plague."

Frau Möller almost smiles. "Touché, Mr. Axelrod." She checks her Sony to be sure it's recording. "Your English is excellent. Where did you learn it?"

"My mother taught *English* English here in Moscow. I earned a master's degree from Columbia University in New York, which is why I speak American English."

Misha, a trainee wearing a shiny polyester suit and a string tie, comes in carrying two cups of coffee and a saucer of sugar on a hubcap doubling as a tray. "And the spoons?" Osip demands.

With a magician's flourish, Misha produces two spoons from his jacket pocket. Laughing under his breath, Osip drops a lump of sugar into each cup and hands one, along with a spoon, to the journalist.

"And what was your discipline at Columbia University?" Adelgunde Möller inquires.

"Soviet history."

"Ah, that explains your Khrushchev story."

Osip stirs his coffee, takes a tentative sip to be sure it is not too hot to drink, then noisily drains the cup. "You could make the case that Soviet history stopped and post-Soviet history began outside my ninth-floor window," he says. "The Russian people toppled the giant statue of the founder of the Soviet Cheka, the late and, at least in Cheka circles, lamented Felix Dzerzhinsky, in front of the Lubyanka Prison. They would have toppled Lenin too. You've probably seen the giant statue in the middle of October Square, a stone's throw from here, of Vladimir Ulyanov, better known as Lenin, surrounded by children, his iron coat billowing in an imaginary wind. The rub, as they say in English English, was that the statue turned out to be too big to topple. So instead of Lenin's statue, the Russian people toppled Lenin's state."

"Which brings us to the post-Soviet era," the journalist observes. "Seen from Berlin, it appears that another plague has descended on Russia. I'm talking about the scavenger capitalists who slaughter each other in the gold rush for riches—something *Pravda* has branded the Great Turf War. I'm talking about your *vory v zakone* who, for a price, supply a roof—not the kind that keeps the rain out but the kind that keeps rival scavenger capitalists out. Your Sixth Bureau of the Organized Crime Control Department, Mr. Axelrod, is tasked with prosecuting the *vory* operating in Moscow and restoring the post-Soviet state's authority. Do you see light at the end of the tunnel?"

Osip sneaks a quick look at his wristwatch. "We are only just now entering the tunnel, Frau Möller," he informs her. "Theoretically, there is said to be light at the end of every tunnel. So, one step at a time, we forge ahead in the expectation of catching a glimpse of it."

"Is the post-Soviet state equipped to fight organized crime?"

"We broke our teeth fighting *dis*organized crime for the last seventy years. There was disorganized crime in every factory and every collective farm and every store that sold consumer goods. It amounted to a shadow economy. When I came to work at the MVD in the early 1980s, there were state farms in Kyrgyzstan growing opium in their fields. *Opium*, Frau Möller, not wheat. Workers struggling to fill state quotas in factories somehow managed to produce battery-powered razors or battery-powered toothbrushes or battery-powered vibrators in the basement, which were smuggled out at night and sold on the black market. People didn't think twice about breaking the law to survive the Sovietization of Russia."

"Are people still breaking the law in order to survive the capitalization of post-Soviet Russia?"

"Look, Frau Möller, with the collapse of the Soviet Union, the entire Russian economy is up for grabs, and the only law governing who gets what is the law of the jungle: Anyone—*vory*, ex-KGB or ex-MVD, ex-convicts, Afghan veterans, local cops, local or regional or national politicians—who can get his hands on consumer goods and deliver them to a market can make a ridiculous pile of money. If—and it's a big if—he doesn't wind up with a bullet in the head in the Great Turf Wars raging in Moscow and other cities. Your sitting in my ninth-floor pigeonhole of an office drinking my ersatz coffee would suggest I'm not telling you anything you don't already know."

"I wanted to hear it from your lips, for the record. Can

you give me an *Übersicht* of the criminal world that exists in Russia today?"

"I don't speak German."

"Excuse me. A *tour d'horizon*."

"I don't speak French either."

"*Lieber Gott*, an overview of the situation in Moscow!"

Kneading his eyebrows to better unpack his memory, Osip begins to deluge the German journalist with details he presumes will baffle her: "The Solntsevskaya Brotherhood—that's spelled *S-O-L-N-T-S-E-V-S-K-A-Y-A*—decided they wanted a piece of Valeri Glugech's lucrative drug-import business. When he made the mistake of refusing, he and two of his senior brigadiers were lured to a meeting at the Rechnoi Vokzal metro station on the Zamoskvoretskaya line, ambushed, and shot dead. The Israelite *pakhan* Naum Caplan is the new boy in town. The criminal groups divided up Moscow before Caplan came on the scene. Now he wants a piece of the action and he seems to have set his sights on Ossete territory. He almost started a turf war with the Ossete *pakhan* Timur the Lame over the Smirnoff Vodka roof. Two days ago there was another incident, this one at a new Porsche dealership—one of Caplan's enforcers wound up with a nine-millimeter bullet lodged in his knee. When the police interviewed the poor son of a bitch at the clinic, he claimed a pistol had gone off by accident during a friendly discussion about territory. This could get ugly before it sorts itself out." Osip glances at the Sony recorder. "You sure you're getting all this? Where was I? Ah, the Kazan *vory* specialize in high-interest loans—when I say *high* I'm talking twenty percent a month and God help the poor bastard who doesn't pony up on time. Do you understand the American expression *pony up*, Frau Möller? *Pony up* as in *fork over*, or *pay up*. Hmmm. The Chechen *vory*, for a stiff fee, escort trucks ferrying European merchandise through the Ukraine to

Moscow. The Azerbaijani *vory* deal in narcotics but are trying to expand, more recently into providing a roof, for a monthly percentage of the profits, to start-up businesses. The problem is that no one in his right mind starts a new business without first organizing a roof, so the Azerbaijani will inevitably wind up stepping on the toes of other *vory*, which means blood will be spilled. The Armenians recently opened a casino in a hotel basement, but that's their way of laundering the profits from their main line of work, which is the theft of automobiles. You can put an order in for, say, a 1990 Mercedes 300SE or BMW E30 Coupe and have the car, with new registration and new license plates and a new paint job if you're not happy with the old paint job, delivered in forty-eight hours. The Georgians, bless their hearts, are into old-fashioned burglaries, with the occasional kidnapping on the side. The Ingush specialize in selling weapons and ammunition—everything from a Stechkin silent revolver to a Dragunov sniper rifle to an AK-47. They are currently peddling Spigot anti-tank missiles, though as our Organized Crime Control Department doesn't have the budget to pay for new cars, much less surplus tanks, I don't see why anyone would waste their hard-earned money on a Spigot. What have I left out? Oh, the Dagestani *vory*, who are the masters of extortion—they have been known to fabricate compromising photographs of politicians or bankers or diplomats and sell the negatives to the people concerned, or their wives, or the press, for a wad of American dollars or German marks or English pounds."

"Can you put numbers to these *vory* gangs, Mr. Axelrod? How many foot soldiers do they have?"

"Nobody knows the size of the Solntsevskaya Brotherhood because, under a very original and very creative franchise scheme, their *pakhan*, for a fee, lets smaller groups pass themselves off as Solntsevo. As for the others, we have a pretty good idea of their numbers, but I don't intend to get into that with you. I don't want this information published. I don't want them to know what we know."

"If you can't put a number to the foot soldiers, perhaps you can tell me how many *vory v zakone* groups are actually out there."

Osip shuffles through the pile of dossiers on his desk, finds the one he is looking for, pries it open. "One of my researchers, pouring over MVD arrest records since the end of the Great Patriotic War, counted two hundred seventy-nine bands of thieves-in-law. How many are still out there is anybody's guess. The reason being that instead of offering protection to what you call scavenger capitalists, many of the *vory* have simply taken over the businesses they protect. When we go after them, we're no longer dealing with gangsters; we're dealing with their lawyers and their accountants, even their public relations people, who accuse us of giving legitimate businessmen a bad name. The old *vory*—the ones who still live by their so-called code of honor—are pretty much extinct." A wry smile elbows its way onto Osip's lips. "Except for one."

"Can you identify the one?"

Osip shrugs. "I suppose there's no harm in telling you. Everyone in the Moscow underworld knows who it is. I'm talking about the Ossete *vory v zakone* presided over by the legendary *pakhan* Timur Monsurov, better known in the street as Timur the Lame." Osip pulls another dossier from the pile but doesn't bother opening it; he doesn't need to. "Timur has done time—twenty-two years in the *zona*, as we euphemistically call our prison camps—but he swears by, and lives by, an outmoded honor code that doesn't guarantee longevity in today's cutthroat Great Turf War."

"Reading between the lines, I can't help feeling you have

a certain respect for this Ossete *vory*. Do you know him personally?"

"I knew his son. He was one of my students the year I lectured at Moscow University."

"What did you lecture on?"

"The Italian mafia."

"Really? That would seem to make you uniquely equipped to suggest what the *vory v zakone* and the mafia have in common."

"They are both criminal organizations."

"And what, given your expertise, Mr. Axelrod, distinguishes these criminal organizations from each other?"

Osip barely manages to keep a straight face. "The mafia thugs speak Italian; our *vory* speak Russian."

Frau Möller's lips compress into a taut smile. "Out of curiosity, are you still in touch with this son of Timur the Lame?"

Osip shakes his head. "Our paths haven't crossed in years. The last I heard he had just come back from England. Our colleagues in MI5 kept careful track of him in London. It wouldn't surprise me to learn that one of their agents sat next to him on the plane."

"Is the son following in the father's footsteps?"

"Excellent question. I don't know the answer." A shadow of doubt clouds Osip's eyes. "The student I knew at the university didn't know the answer either." Osip glances again at his wristwatch. "I'm afraid that's all the time I can give you."

Frau Möller switches off her recorder and slips it into her shoulder bag. "No, you're not."

"I beg your pardon?"

"You're not *afraid* that's all the time you can give me. You are *relieved* that's all the time you can give me." Adelgunde Möller gets up. "I've been around this racetrack before, Mr. Chief of the Sixth Bureau of the Organized Crime Control Department. You were right—you succeeded in not telling me anything I didn't already know. Oh, and by the way, you might alert your trainee, Misha, when he talks to you on the intercom every word he says can be heard in the waiting room. For his information and yours, my hair is naturally dirty blond, I'm wearing a brassiere and pushing forty from the *right* side, thank you." Retrieving her overcoat from the back of the door, she says over her shoulder, "*Einen schönen Nachmittag*, Mr. Axelrod."

Osip, his face a mask of civility, is on his feet. "If you understood what Misha said, it means you were lying when you claimed you don't speak Russian. I, on the other hand, was telling the truth when I told you I don't speak German. I still don't. I never will."

"So, my dear Osip, can I assume you managed to survive the interview with the dreadful Frau Möller with your body, not to mention your ego, more or less intact?" Alexander Smirnov remarks.

Smirnov, the director of the MVD's Organized Crime Control Department and Osip's boss, is polishing off the spider crab he ordered up from the new Japanese restaurant on Gorky Street. Pushing the Styrofoam plate off to the side of his enormous Soviet desk, he wipes his lips on one of the sunflowers printed on his wide silk tie, then melts back into his chair and lights up an Italian cigarette, a third of which is a hollow filter tip. He takes a long, delicious drag on the cigarette, spilling a stream of smoke out through his nostrils. As he eyes Osip over the rims of his spectacles, his nearly bald head is perfectly aligned with the head of Boris Yeltsin in the framed photograph on the wall behind him.

"Frau Möller couldn't repair my coffee machine," Osip informs him. "She's married and was wearing a brassiere. On top of that, she lied about not speaking Russian."

"She's been the *Berliner Zeitung* Moscow correspondent for seven years," the director tells him. "You should have assumed she could speak Russian. It's an old journalist trick of the trade—you pretend not to speak the language, who knows what secrets you can pick up?"

"The only secret she got from me was that the mafia thugs speak Italian and our *vory* gangsters speak Russian," Osip promises.

"Well, let us hope I can pick up more interesting secrets from you. Start with Timur the Lame. So: What precisely do we know about this Ossete *pakhan*?"

"We know he provides the roof for Smirnoff Vodka, for the new Porsche garage number seven, for a handful of hotels and restaurants in Moscow, for three of the new foreign franchises opening for business on Gorky Street, including the Japanese restaurant that delivered your spider crab and that English Sweet Tooth Ltd. candy shop, also for a handful of basement sweatshops manufacturing Western consumer goods in two Moscow suburbs. He doesn't deal in hard drugs or prostitution or surplus Kalashnikovs; he doesn't sell vodka produced from cheap ethyl alcohol imported from Byelorussia; he's not looking to take over a bank or expand his modest protection racket beyond Moscow. In the great scheme of things, Timur the Lame is peanuts compared to the new breed of *bespredel*—the no-holds-barred crowd. On the other hand, he is something of a legend in the *vory* underworld, having survived two stretches in the *zona* with his bogus code of honor intact. My instinct tells me that if we can bring him down, if we can pin a tenner on him and pack him off for another stretch in the *zona*, none of them—the *vory* operating outside the law, the *vory* pretending to operate inside the law and laundering their profits through banks they control or even own—none of them will feel safe. There's another angle to consider, Chief: If we can bring Timur's scalp to Boris

Yeltsin—if we can prosecute him for extortion, for tax evasion, for currency manipulation, for walking around in public with his fly open, whatever—it will establish our Organized Crime Control Department as a force to be reckoned with. Our budget could double or triple overnight, which would enable us to beef up our bureaus with seasoned professionals, and we could keep the staff we have by offering them decent salaries and bonuses. Think of it, Director: We could equip every office with a computer and hire secretaries who know how to work them. We could modernize our fleet of cars so our people don't have to take taxis to arrest the criminals sabotaging the post-Soviet Russian state."

Gripping what is left of the Italian cigarette between his thumb and third finger, Alexander Smirnov positions it in front of his eyes and studies the smoke drifting from the ash as if it contains a coded message. "That's not how I see it," he finally says. "I don't have the manpower—or the patience—to collect Timur's scalp through our legal system."

"Napoleon didn't have the manpower at Waterloo. So he invented a game plan: strategically, one to ten; tactically, ten to one."

"Minor detail: Napoleon lost at Waterloo." Alexander Smirnov stubs out his cigarette in an ashtray filled with filter tips. "There is a better way to bring Timur's scalp to Yeltsin."

"Which is?"

"Bring his *real* scalp on a platter, like John the Baptist's, to Yeltsin."

Osip concentrates on the boss's hair brushed against the grain to cover his balding scalp. "You want me to kill him?" he asks casually.

The director, discomfited at having to explain the obvious, manages a weary smile. "I want you to *let* him be killed.

Knowing Russia, I wouldn't risk my miserable salary betting Timur will survive the law of the jungle raging in Moscow. I read your report about the incident at the Porsche dealership a couple of days ago, where one of Caplan's enforcers took a bullet in the knee and wound up having his leg amputated at a clinic. Caplan will take this personally and want to settle the score. My dear Osip, we need to get out of his way. Let them kill each other off. *Help them kill each other off when you can!*"

"So long as the violence appears to be random—a corpse here, a corpse there—I suppose the bleeding hearts won't lose any sleep," Osip murmurs.

Alexander Smirnov, his nostrils flaring as if he has been ambushed by an unpleasant odor, lapses into a moody silence. His squat body is still glued to the former minister's swivel chair behind the desk but his brain is somewhere else. "What Mother Russia needs to become great again, as we were in the time of Iosif Stalin," he announces, giving himself crucial information, "is more funerals."

9
YULIA: WHEN I FUCK, I STOP TIME DEAD IN ITS TRACKS . . .

PEREDELKINO, A VILLAGE NEAR MOSCOW

A CRUMB OF BACKSTORY BEFORE

PICKING UP THE FRONTSTORY

Here's the thing: I shed my virginity, gleefully, impatiently, triumphantly, at the age of fourteen years, six months, and five days and never looked back. The facilitator was the second deputy director of the Lithuanian branch of the Institute of Experimental Physiology at the Soviet Academy of Sciences, a forty-two-year-old seasonally observant Israelite from Odessa who reeked of aftershave lotion, which obliged me to hold my breath as if I were skin-diving, which in a manner of speaking I was. Seen from a distance either in space or in time, this ritual breaking of the hymen might be thought of as an adolescent's awakening—except that when it happened I was already caffeinated awake, with my eyes wide open memorizing every detail, which I stored up to replay in the inevitable periods of sexual drought. If you're thinking of bringing my second deputy director up on charges of robbing the cradle, forget it. In my mini and push-up bra, I could easily have passed for seventeen, especially if I spoke in the rusty whisper I had perfected talking to my reflection in the bathroom mirror. My mister, the second deputy director, was married and had one son half my age and a mistress twice my age, but hey, he was suitably endowed, and the perfect guide to pilot a neophyte onto the treacherous terra infirma of teenagerhood. In theory I knew what to expect and where to expect it from. You remember my kid cousin, Tzuf, the one who is twelve minutes younger than me? We were in the last grade of primary school and supposed to be doing homework when he and I took it upon ourselves to educate each other in the thing we were most familiar with: our bodies. Which explains why grabbing hold of an erect penis didn't scare the bejesus out of me. Which explains how a howlingly timid Tzuf got his first glimpse of a living, breathing, salivating vagina.

All this happened before my father, the *pakhan* of his Israelite *vory v zakone* in Vilnius, decided he needed a bigger playing field than Lithuania and moved me, my stepmother (Naum Caplan's second but not last wife), his brother Mordechai, and my kid cousin Tzuf, along with his *vory* brigadiers and soldiers, lock, stock, and barrel to Moscow. While my father was putting down roots in the capital and making his first fortune importing computers, he packed me off to a Swiss finishing school, which never quite managed to finish what needed finishing before expelling me when they discovered I was moonlighting weekends as a nude model for a gorgeous young Italian painter named Fabio something. I half-heartedly tried to convince them I was following in the sacred footfalls of our national treasure Anna Akhmatova, who, you'll remember, posed nude for her lover Modigliani in Paris, but the prigs who ran the Swiss penal colony for filthy-rich girls didn't buy into my alibi. I was a month shy of seventeen at the time, but braless with a long silk Sonia Rykiel swirling around my ankles, I could easily pass for twenty-something. Which, to my dad's eternal aggravation, I did. Moscow by night became my feverish stomping ground. Sometimes with my cousin Rosalyn in tow, other times accompanied by young men whose names I never remembered, we baptized the new hard-currency nightclubs that sprouted like mushrooms in out-of-the-way hangars or backstreet hotel basements, literally rubbing shoulders, as we romped to illegal American rock and roll with the Soviet *nomenklatura* who ran the country by day and had money and calories to burn by night. In those wild Moscow years, I was, sexually speaking, (to misuse the *vory* expression) a *bespredel*—a no-holds-barred girl, so long as the fornication in question was consensual. I'll give you a for instance: When I was vacationing in Odessa on one particularly forgettable occasion, an inebriated Party second secretary, beet faced and sweating like a horse from the six hundred grams of Stolichnaya he had polished off over supper, planted himself on our top-floor terrace and, gesturing flamboyantly toward the horizon, offered me the entire Ukraine for my nineteenth birthday. I, clear-headed after having consumed a mere two hundred grams of vodka, reciprocated by offering him a cute Ukrainian, the cigarette girl in the hotel lobby, who, pocketing my one-hundred-US-dollar bill, agreed to join us in our suite for the night.

The very least I could do, having come into possession of the Ukraine, was give him a Ukrainian, you do see that. In my defense—assuming that a defense needs to be deployed—which of us *isn't* a voyeur?

During what I think of as my *bespredel* phase, I did have one vaguely ardent affair. It was with a young junior diplomat on home leave from his post in Madrid. His name was Melor (from *Marx, Engels, Lenin, October Revolution*), which established his pedigree: He came from a long line of Soviet apparatchiki, but as the peasants say, nobody's perfect. Despite the pedigree, he turned out to be creative in bed and funny out of it—a lethal combination when it comes to seduction. On top of which he was as gorgeous as my Italian Modigliani in Switzerland and single and could speak Spanish fluently and dance "Mambo No. 5" with his hips as well as his feet. There was a downside. Alas, there always is. In his case, it was the smile that somehow didn't fit comfortably on his face. It flashed like a neon advert and then vanished without leaving a trace of amusement in the crinkly corners of his eyes. I would have gone along for the ride but two things eventually scared him off. The first was my dad, who would call him my *shegetz* to his face and joke that it was never too late to get circumcised. (You have to know Caplan as well as I do to understand he was half-kidding, half-not.) The second was yours truly: I frightened him off the night he blurted out that he had fallen head over heels in love and proclaimed his determination to be faithful to me, and me alone, until death, hopefully in some far-distant future, did us part. Having exposed the heart on his sleeve, as the saying goes, he gazed at me with those unblinking watery sheepdog eyes men invariably produce when they are under the weather with lovesickness and anticipate central-casting reciprocity. "I am not made to have one lover," I informed him matter-of-factly, "or even one lover at a time." At which point—I'm not making this up—his watery eyes suddenly turned bone dry. To the best of my recollection, "Fuck off" is what he snarled.

The expletive that he neglected to delete marked the end of a curious friendship.

I was not convinced that, me being trapped in me and men being trapped in the straitjacket of their maleness, things would turn out differently with Roman, who, through no fault of his (none of us get to select our parents), happened to be the only son of the legendary *vor* Timur the Lame. On the negative side of the ledger, his being an Ossete with Russian Orthodox ancestors suggested that he probably wasn't circumcised, though this was not a deal-breaker. There is something about the pop-out-pistol-in-your-pocket quirkiness of the uncircumcised penis that I personally find beguiling. Far more serious than not being circumcised, he belonged to the tribe my dad considered to be his arch-enemy. On the positive side, I identified chutzpah (thinking it was possible to have a second chance to make a good first impression) and detected a sense of humor (*Fuck you, Roman from another planet; fuck me, he agreed*). Beyond that my nostrils caught a whiff of desperation, which must have communicated with the seed of desperation in me that I normally repress under a Himalaya of flippancy—how else explain my wanting to see where this might go? Though I was prepared to bail out with or without a parachute at the first sign of unblinking watery sheepdog eyes.

Which brings me to the weekend in Peredelkino.

When I finally managed to escape the wedding reception in the synagogue, I found Roman dozing in the passenger seat of my Porsche. "Been waiting long?" I asked, sliding behind the wheel.

"Twenty-six years," he said.

I remember looking at him as if he had just landed from outer space. "Here's the thing, Roman from another planet: I've had it up to here with peacocks and their fine-feathered phrases. You want to get into my pants. I get that. But stop pretending there is more to it than lust. Lust is all the inspiration you need. You don't have to fake love to justify lust. Don't go there." Shaking my head in bafflement, I thought I needed to yellow in the bottom line: "Like, I'm not a virgin," I informed him. "So carpe diem, Roman from another planet."

"Me also, I'm not a virgin," he shot back. "I'm ready to carpe diem if you are."

I started the motor but we sat there without speaking for a long moment. Then he said something along the lines of "You misunderstand me, Yulia. I'm not pretending. I'm happy to begin whatever we're beginning with lust and move on from there, one foot in front of the other. I'm exploring. I'll settle for less but I'm hoping for more. Since when is hope a crime?"

"Since now," I told him. "Less *is* more than one can expect out of life these days. Assuming you still want to spend the weekend with me, where are we going?"

"A friend of a friend is lending me his dacha at Peredelkino. I'll show you the way."

"I know the goddamn way," I snapped, throwing the car into reverse, backing out of the parking space so fast I left traces of rubber on the pavement, then spinning the wheel and accelerating onto the boulevard. "Been there a dozen times, mostly with peacocks."

Roman, lost in thought, was subdued during the twenty minutes it took us to reach the checkpoint before Peredelkino. Two militiamen wearing thick arctic boilersuits with fur-lined hoods beamed their flashlights into the Porsche from both sides. One of them must have recognized me because he called out, "It's the Caplan kid," as he waved us through. I parked in the field next to the small Orthodox church with a golden dome and followed Roman as he made his way through a maze of winding iron-fenced paths, opening iron gates ahead of us and closing them behind us. At one intersection of paths, he pointed at the tomb of Boris Pasternak in the distance. I could make out the white gravestone in a stand of pine trees. In an undertone that suggested he was talking to himself, he murmured, "I am alone, all around me drowns in falsehood."

I recognized the line from Pasternak's "Hamlet" and finished the poem, which happened to be one of my favorites: "Life is not a stroll across a field."

Roman appeared surprised. "You know the poem?"

"I know that life is not a stroll across a field. Hey, Nadezhda in Moscow, Pasternak in Peredelkino. You seem to have an obsession with gravestones."

"The obsession is with death."

At a gate with the number 45 on a plaque attached to it, Roman reached over the top and threw the latch and let himself in. "There's one more grave you need to see," he said, pointing to the weathered stone jutting from the frozen earth off to the right of the gate. "I promise it will be the last one—for today. It's the tomb of a Soviet soldier named Hippolyte Zhuk, who died defending Peredelkino from the fascists. My friends found his skeleton when they were digging up the garden. He still had a metal dog tag around his ankle so they were able to identify him. It was my friends who put up the stone. Hippolyte's family, what was left of it, came from Byelorussia. There were twelve of them, and they spent an afternoon picnicking next to the grave. We watched from the house while they put apples on the gravestone . . ." Roman turned to look at the weathered two-story dacha with faded red shutters set back in a stand of pines. "They were eating and drinking and laughing and sobbing." He smiled for the first time that day. The smile seemed to sit comfortably on his face. "What do you think of the dacha?" he asked.

"The shutters could use a fresh coat of paint," I told him. "But it will do."

And do it did. We lit roaring fires in the kitchen and bedroom chimneys but both of us kept thick woolen scarves wound around our necks. Roman found a package of spaghetti, a tin of whole tomatoes, and two red onions germinating in a straw basket under the sink and set to work preparing supper. Rummaging through closets, I came up with a bottle of Georgian Mukhrani red. While Roman prepared the pasta sauce, I did what my Swiss finishing-school wardens call a *toilette de chat* in icy water before making my way downstairs gift wrapped (so to speak) in the soft woolen man's bathrobe I found hanging on the back of the bathroom door. "Hmmm, that smells good," I said.

"You smell good," he said.

I educated him. "It's called soap and water. Works every time." He smiled again, and it dawned on me that I had said what I said in the hope of making him smile again.

After supper we fed kindling and logs onto the embers in the bedroom hearth, reigniting the flame—reigniting ours too. We found a linen sheet and pillowcases and a duvet cover in a wooden coffer and, with one of us on each side, made the bed. The four-poster Russian antique creaked when, stark naked except for the scarves around our necks, we finally crawled between the duvet and the sheet, then creaked again as we explored the lust that had brought us to Peredelkino. Later, Roman, sitting up in bed with my bathrobe draped over his shoulder, looked at me strangely as he smoked a cigarette.

"What?"

"Must I embarrass myself by asking?"

"It won't be the first time you embarrassed yourself. So you might as well ask."

"Except for the squeaky bed, it was great for me. How was it for you?"

"It will do," I told him.

"That's it? 'It will do'!"

"Here's the thing: As a general rule it is better, from the female point of view, to keep men unsure of themselves."

He laughed. "It's thanks to me that we're here. At least I get credit for persisting."

"Your persistence was the flip side of your arrogance. Don't get on your high horse. Like most males, you are infected with a reasonable amount of arrogance, Roman. I don't mind a crumb of arrogance in men. It's a weakness that a woman can exploit."

"You're planning to exploit what you identify as my weakness?"

"You already exploited what you surely identified as my weakness."

"What weakness of yours did I exploit?"

"My appetite for sex. I like to fuck, Roman. When I fuck, I stop time dead in its tracks. When I finish fucking, I am precisely the same age as when I started fucking. Not a second, not a minute, if the fucking lasted, not an hour older."

I could see him mulling this. "If you're fortunate," he finally said, "you will grow old one day."

"Not if I can continue stopping time in its tracks."

"No wonder your parents nicknamed you Scapegrace." When he noticed my surprise he said, "Rosalyn told me. You remember Rosalyn, don't you?"

I wasn't sure I appreciated his throwing my *You remember Rosalyn, don't you?* back in my face, given that I had just made love with her lover. "Of course I remember my cousin Rosalyn," I said. "We were sent off to Vladimir Lenin All-Union Pioneer camp together the summer we turned fifteen. When her father, Caplan's younger brother, my uncle Mordechai, discovered Rosalyn had lost her virginity, he made a stink, accusing me of being a bad influence on his daughter. Me, a bad influence! I don't deny that I more or less pushed her into the muscular arms of one of the swimming instructors, a Uighur with a shaved scalp and gorgeous Oriental eyes and a sumptuous rust-colored mustache, persuading her she had nothing to lose except, with any luck, her virginity. *Scapegrace* got pinned on me because of mischief I got into."

"What kind of mischief?"

"Innocent stuff like sex, not your *vory* mischief like murder."

The flickering flames and the shadows playing on the walls must have drugged me because I drifted into a deep sleep. I remember dreaming I was falling past stars, my arms stretched ahead of me as if I were plunging off a diving board into a pool, except that there was no deliciously sensuous splash of water at the end of the dive—only a splash of quicksilver from the thickness of the Milky Way that lightened the blackness of space. When I opened my eyes, the first smidgen of first light was tinting the bedroom's french window. Roman was fast asleep, his lips parted as if for a kiss, his head buried in the pillow. Slipping out of bed, I wrapped the bathrobe around myself and padded barefoot to the window to watch the dawn break. A shard of moon was glistening in the carpet of stars I had just fallen through. Suddenly, I became aware of Roman, stark naked, behind me. Pushing the long strands of my hair and the single braid to one side, he pressed two fingers to my neck as if he were feeling for a pulse, then slipped around in front of me. I fumbled with the belt of the bathrobe but before I could open it he folded his body into mine. Forgetting the belt, I flung my arms around his neck and pressed my warm body into his shivering body. After a moment he backed off. "For me," I heard him murmur, "time doesn't stop in its tracks—it races to keep up with my racing heart." I reached down and wrapped my polar fingers around his Sahara penis and touched my lips to the small tattoo on his chest: a naked angel with her wings spread to protect the flame of a candle from the wind. "Your tattoo is beautiful," I whispered.

"In my father's time the *vory* were called *sinie*, the blue ones, because of their tattoos."

"Aside from fucking you, so far the thing I like most about you is your tattoo. Identify the flame that your blue angel is protecting."

"Yulia Naumovna is the name of the flame."

"Another of your peacock phrases," I snapped. But I fear I failed to keep the satisfaction out of my voice or the smile out of my eyes.

10
NAUM CAPLAN: WHEN YOU PAY SOMEONE BACK, ADD INTEREST . . .

MOSCOW

Sunday, January 12, 1992

Folded snugly into an Italian parka lined with raccoon, the hood pulled over his balding head, Naum Caplan climbs the spiral steel stairs and opens the thick steel door to the roof garden of the Narodnaya Hotel. He has leased the two top floors of the sixteen-floor building in the heart of Moscow's Jewish Quarter since it opened for business two years ago, as well as a corner of one of the subbasement parking levels for the family's seven cars and Yulia's new Porsche, along with the two Studebaker armored personnel carriers—relics from the Great Patriotic War, one of which works, the second of which needs a new Studebaker carburetor that no longer exists, at least not in Russia. The lease also includes a dedicated express elevator manned by one of Caplan's enforcers, who takes a perverted pleasure in frisking visitors, especially females, to make sure they are not carrying. Caplan, who recently turned seventy-four, doesn't appreciate Moscow winters as much as his daughter, Yulia, but since relocating from

Vilnius, he has learned to live with the stinging subzero temperatures and the ankle-deep snow that sticks until spring. He has had the recent snowfall shoveled off the roof garden and prefers to meet with his brigadiers here when they are plotting a necktie party. His younger brother, Mordechai, and Mordechai's son, Tzuf, are waiting for him on the raised wooden part of the roof with its empty pigeon hutches. Looking out at the great Marina Roscha Synagogue across Vysheslavtsev Lane, Caplan makes a mental note to check that his monthly sweetener has been delivered to the rabbi. Doing whatever it takes to stay in the good graces of local community leaders is a long-standing reflex. Lest anyone accuse him of sectarianism, he also sends a monthly envelope to the local Orthodox patriarch.

"Brother, I don't like the cold or the view from the roof," Mordechai, who served four years of an eight-year sentence for manslaughter before profiting from a Victory Day amnesty, says. "Why can't we meet downstairs in a room with radiators like civilized Muscovites?"

"There are no civilized Muscovites in Moscow," Caplan informs him. "It is well known that all the civilized Muscovites live in Leningrad. The problem with a room with radiators, brother, walls are known to have ears."

"Uncle Naum, who is the condemned *vor* in your sights?" inquires Tzuf, a veteran Red Army sniper who served two back-to-back six-month tours in Afghanistan perfecting the fine art of slaughtering mujahideen at a thousand meters.

"What makes you think I have someone in my sights?"

"When you meet us on the roof, you always have someone in your sights, Uncle."

Caplan sniffs at the icy air, which tickles his nostrils. "You have more experience than most looking through sights, nephew. It's the Ossete sixer they call the Argentine."

"The one who went and shot our guy in the knee at the Porsche garage?"

"One and the same," Caplan says. "There is method to my madness: If our enemies suppose that I am a crazy Jew who believes in an eye for an eye, it will give us an advantage in the turf war. My guy lost his leg. I want the Argentine to lose his leg. Shoot a bullet into his knee; make sure it's the left one. Timur the Lame will get the message about my madness even if the Organized Crime Control clowns don't. When you have done that, I want you to shoot a bullet through his eye into his brain."

"Left or right eye?" Tzuf demands with a straight face. Seeing his uncle's reaction, he quickly says, "Just joking, Uncle."

"Brother," Mordechai remarks, "shooting him in the eye is more than a knee for a knee."

"When you pay someone back, my brother, you must be careful to add interest," Caplan instructs him.

"The Ossetes sure bend your nose out of joint," Tzuf says.

"Their *pakhan* humiliated me. I was not looking to start a *razborka* over Smirnoff Vodka. I would have met him halfway, but he is a prisoner of his prison culture. For him, there is no halfway."

"You want my opinion," Tzuf says, "if we're looking for turf, the Chechens would roll over like a dog scratching fleas."

"When I want your opinion, nephew, I will ask for it. As for the Argentine, here is what you need to know to deliver my knee for a knee with interest."

Lice and Spare Rib and the Greek wrap themselves in white terry-cloth bathrobes and, water dripping from their bare feet, pad from the old tsarist-era *banya* to the private Turkish dining room next to it. The Argentine, who has put on weight and sprouted a drooping walrus mustache since becoming one of

Timur's enforcers, dips one last time in the wooden tub filled with ice water, then, shaking himself like a dog, collects his bathrobe and trails after his three friends. Lounging on one of the low Turkish couches with bath towels spread across them, Lice reaches over the folds of his sumo stomach and hits the button on the intercom. "We're ready for zakuski, Dmitri," he calls into the speaker. "And don't fucking forget the double helping of blinis. Last Thursday your people forgot the extra blinis."

"Extra blinis and extra salmon will be on the cart," a voice calls back. "On our way up now."

"Who the fuck was that?" the Argentine, suddenly alert, demands. "I didn't recognize the voice."

"It sure wasn't Dmitri," the Greek says. "Maybe his shift ended at six."

"Hey, the whole purpose of a sauna is to relax," Spare Rib says. "It's probably that new guy they hired last week."

The Argentine, who has been jumpy since the shooting at the Porsche garage—not to mention the very public dressing down he got from Timur for being trigger-happy—retrieves the stubby PSM semiautomatic from his knapsack and, punching the magazine home, stashes it under one of the small cushions behind his back. There is a knock on the door. "See who it is before you throw the bolt," the Argentine tells Lice.

Lice pushes aside the round cover on the peephole and looks out. Snorting, he says, "It's the zakuski cart."

"You recognize the guys pushing it?" the Argentine asks.

"I recognize the zakuski," Lice says irritably. "Or you want to eat or you don't want to eat."

"Let them in, for fuck's sake, before I die of starvation," Spare Rib says.

Shrugging, Lice throws the bolt. The Argentine reaches under the cushion for his pistol as two men, wearing the white trousers and white sweaters and white gloves of sauna attendants, plant themselves under the door's metal detector. Lice looks up at the red bulb, which remains unlit. "They're clean," he announces, waving for them to come in. Seeing the unlit bulb, the Argentine relaxes his grip on the pistol. One of the attendants pushes the cart filled with zakuski and two bottles of iced vodka into the room. The other attendant shuts the door behind him—and then bolts it closed.

The Argentine sits up. "Why the fuck did he bolt the door?" he demands. "You—yeah, you—why the fuck did you bolt the door?"

The attendant flashes an innocent grin. "We figured you fellows, being that you're Ossetes, would enjoy your zakuski more if the door was bolted when you eat, is all," he says. With a flourish that catches everyone's attention, the second attendant lifts the silver cover on the oval serving dish, revealing a side of salmon. "This fish was swimming in the Baltic yesterday," he announces. The first attendant lifts the bulbous cover on the large round serving dish, revealing two Nagant revolvers fitted with home-tooled silencers fashioned from yellow tennis balls. In a split second one of the revolvers is in his fist, covering the four Ossetes as he flips the second revolver to his partner.

"I told you I didn't recognize the fucking voice," the Argentine whines.

The attendant standing over the Baltic salmon peels the tinted glasses from his face and the beard from his chin. "I know you," the Argentine says. "I know the fucker," he tells the others.

"Tzuf Caplan, in the flesh," Tzuf says.

Lice spreads his hands wide, palms up. "Is this something we can work out?"

Tzuf purses his lips. "You three are okay. It's the Argentine who is in water over his head."

The Argentine, his voice reduced to a rasping whisper, says, "The Greek here is the keeper of our *obshchak*. Name the amount of money you need to make this go away, the Greek will organize it. Isn't that right, Greek?"

"Listen, you guys, if it's a question of money . . ." The Greek doesn't finish the sentence.

"You're not thinking clearly," Tzuf tells the Argentine. "Listen up. There are half a dozen roles I see myself playing in life: Soviet Army sniper, mafia don, stand-up comic, English country gentleman, Latin lover in Italian films, even *banya* attendant on special occasions."

"This here sure qualifies as a special occasion," Tzuf's partner jokes.

"The role I am most comfortable with," Tzuf goes on, "is the English gentleman. All things being equal, I would challenge you to a duel—swords, daggers, pocketknives, baseball bats, water pistols filled with acid at ten paces—in the grand old style when men worth their salt valued their honor more than their lives. But we live in different times, don't we, Argentine? Gentlemen are a vanishing breed. Those of us who have survived this new Russian ice age cannot afford to abandon brutality if we are interested in longevity. Do you have a Christian name, Argentine? The one they will put on your tombstone when they bury you?"

"Argentine is how I'm called. I don't remember my Christian name."

"Well, Argentine, my friend here and me, we were born into the Israelite faith. Whether we pronounce the sacred name of Yahweh correctly in the holy of holies once a year is beside the point. We believe in the Torah. We believe in the commandment that instructs us *a knee for a knee*."

The blood drains from the Argentine's lips as he grasps what is about to happen. Remembering the PSM, he starts to slide his hand under the cushion, but his fingers tremble so violently Tzuf can't miss it. "To quote the unforgettable words of the Argentine," he says, gesturing with his pistol for him to desist, "you don't want to go there unless you need another buttonhole in your bathrobe pocket."

The Argentine desists.

Snickering to himself, Tzuf inquires, "Not that it will change anything, but do you have a preference?"

The Argentine wipes sweat from his forehead with the back of a wrist. "Preference?"

"Which knee?"

"Fuck you, fuck the seep of your sperm for seven generations."

"If you're trying to make me angry, you are wasting your breath. I do not need to be angry to do what I am going to do." Tzuf tightens the silencer on the cannon of his pistol. "It's just as well you do not have a preference, being as I do . . ." He stretches out his arm, lining up the Nagant with the Argentine's left knee, and trips the hair trigger. There is a soft whistle that sounds like air escaping from a punctured tire as the 7.62mm cartridge, its blunt nose nicked so it would fragment on impact, shatters the sixer's kneecap.

Drowning in tears spilling from his eyes, the Argentine gasps for breath. "That . . . makes . . . us . . . even," he manages to say.

"Regrettably for you, we did not come here to get even," Tzuf informs him. "We came here to deliver a knee for a knee—with interest." And he raises his arm and shoots another 7.62mm cartridge into the Argentine's left eye, which suddenly ceases to exist.

Lice turns away and covers his face with a towel. The Greek vomits into the basket filled with spare towels. Spare Rib, his mouth gaping open as he gulps air into his lungs, blurts between painful hiccups, "What the—*hiccc*—fuck, you—*hhiccc*—probably—*hicccp*—probably—*hhhicccp*—*killed him*!"

"I probably did," Tzuf agrees pleasantly. "I offed twenty-nine during my two tours in Afghanistan. The late Argentine makes it an even thirty."

Lice, his fleshy sumo wrestler's body jammed onto the straight-backed kitchen chair with the two front legs sawed off shorter to make it uncomfortable, sits with his head bent, the palms of his hands over his ears not so much to dampen sound as to prop up his head, which after hours of questioning feels heavy. "I told you once, I told you a hundred times," Lice complains. "The guy who shot the Argentine was African, black as the night outside your window over there."

Osip Axelrod exchanges smirks with his trainee, who is leaning against the wall behind Lice. "Consider the possibility he didn't hear the question, Chief," Misha says. "If he takes his hands off his ears, he might come up with a smarter answer."

"I hear real well," Lice says. "It's two in the morning and then some. I been answering your questions since you brought me in, which by my count is five hours ago. I cannot keep my eyes open. I need to sleep."

"You were at the Porsche garage when one of Caplan's *vory* took a bullet in the knee," Osip reminds him.

Lice manages to nod.

"The Argentine was there also, right?"

"I told you—it was a friendly conversation between two *vory* about who would do the roof of the garage."

"If it was so friendly, how come Caplan's *vor* got shot in the knee and wound up minus one leg?"

"He was showing us his new pistol. Then the Argentine

showed him his old pistol. Then the guy asks if he could feel its weight. He must have thought the safety was on because it went off all by itself when he took hold of it."

Osip laughs under his breath. "You actually expect an adult human to believe this cockamamie story?"

Lice shrugs. "All I can tell you officers is what I seen."

Osip Axelrod makes his way to the room next to his office, shutting the door behind him. One of his agents, wearing the uniform of a frontier guard, stands next to a watercooler, his eyes fixed on the lean Ossete *vor* known as Spare Rib and the older Ossete *vor* known as the Greek. "Tell me again what the shooter looked like," he orders for Osip's benefit.

Spare Rib, his voice hoarse, his eyes dark with fright, groans. "I badly need to piss," he says.

"Piss in your pants," the agent says.

Osip repeats the agent's question. "Identify the shooter."

"Like I told you, he was an Uzbek—round face, slanty eyes."

"Your pal in the other room says the shooter was a Negro."

The Greek looks up. "The second guy with the Uzbek, he could have been a Negro, I never got a good look at him. My attention was all the time on the shooter."

"Do you need me to stimulate their memory, Osip?" the agent asks.

Osip shakes his head. "Let them stew in their lies," he remarks. Returning to his office, he kicks the back leg of the kitchen chair to get Lice's attention. "Spare Rib and the Greek claim the shooter was an Uzbek," he says.

"Now that I think of it, the second guy looked a lot like an Uzbek. But the one what shot the Argentine was coal black."

Osip settles onto the edge of his desk. "I want to ask you a hypothetical question, Lice. You understand the word *hypothetical*? If you could get up from the chair and walk out of this building and take a taxi to the airport, and you could get an airplane to anyplace in the world, where would you go?"

Lice perks up. Is this Osip character offering him a way out? "Anyplace at all?"

"Anyplace," Osip confirms. "Australia. South Africa. Mexico. Brazil. New York. You name it."

"I would catch a flight to Tbilisi. I would get my cousin Khetag, who teaches primary school there, to drive me the hundred kilometers to Tskhinvali, which is where I grew up, which is where I won the local sumo-wrestling silver medal when I was sixteen. My old man owns a small farm on a hill over the Liakhvi River. On stifling summer days, us kids would swim in it after we brought in the cows from the field. At night we would sweet-talk girls from the village into climbing to the grassy hummock above the river. There was nights when the Milky Way was so close you could reach out and touch it with your fingertips."

Osip nods agreeably. "You bring in my cows, Lice, I'll bring in yours."

Misha reads from a typed report. "It was the Argentine who shot Caplan's guy in the knee at the Porsche garage? It was Caplan's nephew, Tzuf, who yelled, 'This isn't going away!' when they carried Caplan's guy to their pickup?"

Osip picks up where Misha left off. "You're asking us to swallow that one of Caplan's soldiers gets himself shot in the left knee when both the Argentine and Tzuf were at the Porsche garage. A few days later the Argentine gets himself shot in the same knee. That's one hell of a coincidence. Someone is sending us a message, Lice."

Lice snickers. "There are things that are a discoincidence."

"*Dis*coincidence?" Osip repeats. "Like what?"

"Come on," Lice says. He shifts his considerable weight on

the kitchen chair, trying to find a comfortable position. "Like Caplan's guy didn't get hisself shot in the left eye but the Argentine did. That there's a discoincidence."

Osip comes around behind the chair and talks into Lice's ear. "Tzuf was the shooter, wasn't he? Two chefs in the sauna kitchen described the bearded guy who took the tray up: He was young; he was thin as a vegetarian on a hunger strike; his hair was down to his neck and flecked with gray, which was curious for someone his age; he sported a beard that looked as if it had been glued onto his jaw. You would only be telling us what we already know, Lice. It was Tzuf who shot the Argentine, first in the knee, then in the eye, wasn't it?"

Lice twists around to look at his tormenter. "You need to know where I come from, Mr."—he glances at the wooden plaque on the desk—"Mr. Initial-O Axelrod. I did time with the *pakhan* Timur in Strict Regime Corrective Labor Colony Number Forty. I been with him in and out of the *zona* since. I give you the time of day, I am signing my death certificate."

"The Organized Crime Control Department has a witness-protection program. We can give you a new identity," Osip says. "A new internal passport, a ticket back to Tskhinvali, enough money to buy yourself your own farm on the Liakhui. Finger Tzuf and we will settle the score for the Ossete *vory v zakone*."

"If a score needs to be settled—mind you, I am not saying one does—our *pakhan* Timur will take care of the matter. Anything else would be dishonorable."

"You give my boss what he needs, Lice, he will set you up for life," Misha says from the wall.

"I give him what he needs, he will be setting *me* up for death." Lice puts his hands back over his ears. "The guy who shot the Argentine was an African, black as the night outside your fucking window."

Misha says, "You're dealing with a mule, Chief."

"I may be a mule," Lice mutters, "but I'm a live mule."

Osip wastes another ten minutes trying to convince Lice to turn state's evidence, then gives up and motions with the back of his hand for him to collect his friends and leave. "It's the damn *vory v zakone* code," Osip explains to his trainee. "In or out of the *zona*, they were not permitted to lift a little finger to help the Communists. The habit, like cocaine addiction, is hard to break. They are not about to help us solve a murder now that the Communists are reduced to sawdust being swept into the trash bin." Osip shuts his eyes and rubs the lids with his fists. "Wouldn't change much if one of them did finger Tzuf," he tutors Misha. "You can count on him having an ironclad alibi—half a dozen *vory* and their girlfriends, who will swear on a stack of Bibles he was at an orgy when the Argentine lost his eye."

"If you knew that all along, why did you go to the trouble of interrogating them?"

"Good question. I suppose."

"You *suppose*?"

Osip retrieves his coat from the metal hanger in the closet. "I suppose I keep hoping there must be another way to deal with the *vory v zakone* than . . ."

"Than?"

"You don't want to know."

11
TIMUR THE LAME: IF WORD SPREADS THAT CAPLAN GOT AWAY WITH KILLING ONE OF OURS, OTHERS WILL SMELL BLOOD . . .

MOSCOW

Monday, January 13, 1992

Timur stares out the window at Moscow, shrouded in thick winter fog. Not for the first time he regrets the mansion was built so far back from the road that the sound of traffic doesn't reach his ears. Now, two hours or so before first light, because of the fog even the city's light doesn't reach his eyes. Rasputin, standing just inside the door of Timur's private apartment, uneasily shifting his weight from one foot to the other, says, "The least you guys could have done was get your stories straight."

Lice and Spare Rib, sitting stiffly on the couch, exchange looks. "In our defense, when the Crime Control coppers interrogated us," Lice says, "they kept us in separate rooms. I did not have no way of knowing what the others was going to tell them."

"Which is how come you wound up telling them the killer was an African Negro and Spare Rib and the Greek claimed he was an Uzbek with Oriental eyes," Roman says.

"Which is how come," Lice allows.

Timur turns from the window. "You never mentioned Tzuf's name?"

"None of us never said his name," Spare Rib swears. "He was the one what brought it up."

"Who was *he*?" Roman asks.

"The other interrogator, the one wearing a uniform, called him Osip," Spare Rib remembers.

"O. Axelrod," Lice says. "I seen his name written on a piece of wood on his desk."

"What did he say about Tzuf?" Rasputin demands.

"He said it was a hell of a coincidence that one of Caplan's soldiers gets hisself shot in the left knee when both the Argentine and Tzuf was present at the Porsche garage," Lice says, "and now the Argentine goes and gets hisself shot in the same knee a couple of days later."

Spare Rib elbows Lice in the ribs. "He could not have got hisself shot in the *same* knee, dumbass. Each one of 'em got shot in his *own* knee."

"That is what he must've meant, for shit's sake," Lice says.

"What did you say when he talked about it being a coincidence?" Timur asks.

"I told him there was also things that are a discoincidence. I told him Caplan's guy didn't get hisself shot in the left eye but the Argentine did."

Rasputin rolls his own eyes in disgust. "Smart," he mutters.

"What did I do wrong, for fuck's sake?" Lice pleads.

"Getting born was the first thing you did wrong," Rasputin says.

"Take it slow and easy, Mika," Timur tells Rasputin. "We are all on edge. You boys go find the Greek. He needs commiseration. He's taking the Argentine's death pretty hard."

The two climb to their feet. Lice starts to say something, then, shaking his head, thinks better of it.

"Spit it out," Rasputin orders.

Lice concentrates on his stomach, which spills over his thick belt. "We thought these guys was there about the knee," he says. "We did not know—"

"Even if we was to know," Spare Rib puts in, "there was nothing we coulda done, *pakhan*. The both of them, they had artillery—"

"I am not blaming you," Timur tells them. "The Argentine does not stop to think twice at the Porsche garage. Then this Tzuf character—from what I hear he is crazy—he does not stop to think twice at the *banya*. Things happen. You did good not telling the cops about Tzuf. He is our problem, not theirs. We will deal with it." Timur gestures toward the door. Lice and Spare Rib nod their thanks. When they are gone, Timur settles into the seat behind his desk. "Does the Argentine have family?" he asks Rasputin.

"A father in a village in Georgia. Assuming she is still alive, his mother's mother in Buenos Aires—she's the one he was visiting when he got impressed into the Argentine army for six years."

Timur issues instructions to Rasputin. "When the cops release the body, get the Greek to pay for transporting it back to the father in Georgia. Pay for the funeral also. Tell the Greek not to stint on the coffin—I want to give the Argentine a good send-off. And the Greek needs to organize the usual compensation for the father."

"I am on it, *pakhan*."

"I want you to double the number of sixers on duty downstairs at any one time. Make sure they are armed with automatic pistols and spare magazines. Pay careful attention to the crowd that turns up in the morning. Everyone is to be body searched;

their baskets and rucksacks need to be searched; the diapers of babies need to be searched."

"How about I install a metal detector at the door like they are putting in at airports, *pakhan*?"

"Lot of good that did the Argentine," Roman says under his breath.

"A metal detector cannot hurt," Timur decides. "Having to pass through a detector can make someone think twice about hitting us here." He looks at Roman, who is straddling a kitchen chair back to front. "As of now, my darling son, we are at war," he announces. "Total war. If Caplan had settled for a knee for a knee, we would have something to talk about. But an eye when there is no previous eye!" He turns back to Rasputin. "I want to see a list of Caplan's brigadiers and foot soldiers. I want to see where they hang their hats. I want to see where they come from. If they have done time, I want to know where and for what. I want everything you can get on the top two floors of the Narodnaya Hotel: the access by elevator or stairs, also the access to his subbasement parking, how many cars he has, which makes. And I want a list of Caplan's family."

"I've been saving string on Caplan since he turned up in Moscow," Rasputin says with a smug grin. "Not counting the new Porsche he bought his daughter, he has seven cars stashed in the hotel's first subbasement, along with two army-surplus personnel carriers, one of which is missing a piece from the motor and does not work. The garage is guarded twenty-four seven by retired cops. When Caplan goes somewhere, he always rides in the back of the Studebaker that does work, so it will be next to impossible to organize a hit. A bazooka would only scratch the Studebaker's armor. We would need to plant a bomb on his route, but for that we would need to know what route his Studebaker takes—which is why he never takes the same route twice when he puts his big toe outside the hotel. As for family, he has a younger brother, name of Mordechai; he has that prick of a nephew, Mordechai's only son, Tzuf; he has a niece, Mordechai's daughter and Tzuf's sister, name of Rosalyn; he has a daughter, name of Yulia. From all reports, she is—"

Roman interrupts Rasputin. "I think we need to leave family out of this."

Timur looks at his son. "Why? Tzuf was the shooter. It's a little late to leave him out of this."

"I meant the girls," Roman says. "They had nothing to do with the murder of the Argentine."

"How do we know that?" Rasputin demands.

"Rosalyn is not on talking terms with her uncle," Roman says. "As for Yulia, she's a creature from a Swiss finishing school, for Christ's sake. She's a spoiled kid. The love of her life at the moment is the Porsche her father gave her for her birthday." Roman snickers knowingly at his friend. "As someone who has fallen in love with his Range Rover, you ought to relate to that, Mika."

Rasputin ignores Roman's gibe. "This Yulia didn't finish finishing school," he tells the *pakhan*. "She got herself booted out for extracurricular sex." Suddenly, a light goes off in his brain, and he twists around to scowl at Roman. "Tell me she wasn't the female in the Porsche parked outside the Porsche dealership!"

Timur looks from one to the other. "Nobody said anything to me about a Porsche outside the dealership."

Roman turns to his father. "The girls have got nothing to do with Tzuf shooting the Argentine and our turf war with Caplan."

Timur considers the matter. "Tzuf," he finally decides, "is number one on our hit list. His father, this Mordechai, is fair game. Caplan is fair game. His brigadiers and enforcers and foot soldiers are fair game. For the time being we will leave the daughter and the niece be."

"How do you see this playing out, *pakhan*?" Rasputin asks.

"I see us picking the principals off one by one. There is a lot more riding on this than turf. Our reputation is at stake here. If word spreads that Caplan got away with killing one of ours, others will smell blood and come in for a piece of the carcass." Timur glances at his watch. "See to the security of the mansion," he tells Mika. "When you have taken care of that, we will figure out our next move."

Rasputin understands that the *pakhan* wants a word with his son; he has a good idea about what. "I'll be downstairs if you need me," he announces as he heads for the door.

Timur comes around the desk and pulls up a chair facing Roman, their knees almost touching. "What is it with you and these Jew girls?" he demands.

"Consider the possibility that what attracts me to them is that it rubs you the wrong way."

"If it makes you feel more of a man to rebel against your father, fine, but find another way to do it."

"Anyway, it's over between me and Rosalyn," Roman says.

"And the other one, the Jew girl with the Porsche, who, if I have it right, happens to be the daughter of the Jew Caplan?"

"With her, I'm not sure it ever really began."

"Make sure it stays unbegun. Find yourself a nice Ossete girl who can give you sons."

"The way you did, Father?"

"You could do worse than follow in my footsteps, my darling son." He gestures at the four floors of the mansion beneath his feet. "I have not done badly for an Ossete from Areshperani."

"You have come a long way from Areshperani, I am the first to admit it. Looking back, do you ever wake up in the middle of the night wishing you were a shepherd in the mountains of Georgia instead of the *pakhan* of a band of Ossetes shipwrecked in Moscow?"

Timur pushes himself to his feet and begins to pace back and forth, as if hoping to walk off an inner turmoil before his son notices it. In the end the turmoil erupts. "I am not sure I appreciate your question," he says softly. He spins on the heel of his lame foot and repeats what he said, but louder. "I do not appreciate your question, much less the tone in which you ask it. You have somehow succeeded in convincing yourself you are superior to me because you don't have blood on your hands. When I was your age, Roman, there were only two ways to stay alive, two ways to get ahead, and both involved blood on your hands. You could become a member of their lovely Communist Party, which turned you into one kind of criminal. Or you could become an honest criminal and live by the *vory* code. I chose the second. It suited my nature to be outside looking in. It was a ticket for my adopted Ossete family to survive, even to thrive." Timur stops abruptly and gazes down at Roman. "To answer your insolent, not to mention disrespectful, question, my darling son: I almost never wake up in the middle of the night. On the very few occasions when I do and look over my shoulder, I am not weighed down by regrets. And I certainly do not feel shipwrecked."

Rising, Roman reaches for his father's hand, but Timur, uncomfortable with any display of emotion, quickly pulls it back. Roman, cringing inwardly at the rebuke, blurts out, "I used the word without thinking, my father." He hesitates, then plunges. "With all respect, you have not understood the dynamic between us. Not long ago you told me the past is never past. I took that to mean you never left Strict Regime Corrective Labor Colony Number Forty. Your body is here in Moscow but your head is back on the Perm steppe. You are still the *pakhan* in the windowless attic listening to a poet read Pushkin for a crust of bread. You were condemned to ten years at Labor Colony Number

Forty, but it turned out to be a life sentence. You can never get out. And if, like me, you are outside of Labor Colony Number Forty, you can never get in. That's the wall between us, Father. Does this make sense to you?"

Breathing noisily through his good nostril, Timur turns his back on his son and hobbles toward the door. "No," he mutters angrily. "No sense. None at all."

"Oh God, Father, how do you not see it? You keep track of the time in Areshperani; I need to know the time in Moscow!"

Timur slams the door behind him.

12
TIMUR THE LAME: THE PENAL ANTHILL SO GLACIAL EVEN SUNSHINE FELT COLD AGAINST THE SKIN . . .

VORKUTA GULAG, INSIDE THE ARCTIC CIRCLE

The backstory

The hard truth that Timur couldn't ignore after his first arrest (not to mention the three broken fingers) at the tender age of fourteen was, if you can't run faster than two middle-aged potbellied plainclothes detectives, forget about a career as a pickpocket. Which explains why, in his seventeenth year, he stumbled into a lucrative scam that didn't require forward motion faster than a walk: fabricating two-hundred-year-old Orthodox icons. He had rented a maid's room in a prerevolution building near the Maïakovskaïa metro from Estonian sisters who, as luck would have it, were skillful forgers. They were counterfeiting official birth certificates, death certificates, divorce certificates, and the occasional Moscow residence permit when Timur managed to convince them they were squandering their talents. He swiped a book of icons from the library annex of an Orthodox church and set the sisters to work. After some trial and error mixing Prussian blue and alizarin with egg yolk, they were able to produce remarkable copies of Saint George and the Dragon, Noah and the Ark, and, once they had mastered the incandescence of flame, Moses and the burning bush. Timur would stash the freshly painted panels of wood on the roof of an alleyway outhouse for a month or two of exposure to the elements, then varnish the weathered product and peddle his wares in the lobbies of swanky watering holes frequented by Western tourists. The several times a house detective caught him in the act, the gift of one or two icons would persuade the officer of the law to look the other way while Timur broke the law.

At the age of twenty-two Timur branched out into caviar, packaging black beluga in kilo tins at a sweatshop he'd set up in the basement of a neighborhood grocery store and selling them to embassies for half the price Petrossian charged in Paris. Ironically, when he was finally arrested—it was in 1941; he had just turned twenty-four—it had nothing to do with icons or caviar but everything to do with his being Ossete. In the wake of the German invasion, in June of that year, Stalin—a practicing paranoiac who saw enemies, real or imagined, everywhere—had ordered the Red Army to "cleanse" Russia west of the Urals of indigenous peoples that he feared, given half a chance, might be tempted to collaborate with the Wehrmacht. Which is how Timur found himself, along with thousands of Kalmyks, Karachai, Chechens, Ingush, ethnic Germans, and Ossetes, deported in the winter of 1941 to the Vorkuta Gulag, one of more than a hundred penal anthills a day's reindeer sled ride inside the Arctic Circle on the Vorkuta tundra so glacial even sunshine felt cold against the skin. Timur was assigned to a long, low brick barrack with slit windows covered in rawhide, set upwind from enormous stacks spewing threads of black smoke into the permafrost wasteland. The *vor* who ran the barrack, Kosta Karatsev, an arthritic old man in the twelfth year of a twenty-year sentence for the murder of his wife's lover, turned out to be an Ossete from the same village on the Caspian Steppe as Timur—Areshperani in Georgia's eastern region of Kakheti. Interrogating the new *zek* to be sure he wasn't a stool pigeon or, worse still, a Communist, Kosta discovered the link and took the lame Timur under his wing. He assigned him to a bunk that had the name of a previous occupant beautifully carved on one of its wooden cross boards: Igor Poznanski. "I recollect Poznanski," Kosta told his protégé one night. "He was Leon Trotsky's secretary in the twenties. In 1938 they carted poor Igor off to a tundra and shot him and dumped his body in an unmarked trench in the frozen earth, so one of the guards told me when Poznanski didn't turn up for the morning roll call. You were fortunate to be executed in winter, because if the bullet didn't kill you the cold would. Executions in summer were a calamity. The guards were usually drunk, and as some of the condemned prisoners were only wounded, the earth they bulldozed onto the bodies would still be moving the next day. Stick with me like a shadow, my son, and you won't end up with a bullet in the back of the neck." To prove his point, Kosta had Timur issued a pair of reindeer-hide boots, one of which was fitted with an extra-thick sole and heel, then arranged for him to be tattooed with the telltale portrait of Lenin on his right breast (*Vladimir Organizer of Revolution*, or *thief*) and inducted into the colony's *vory v zakone*. On one of those miserably bleak Arctic mornings when the nights last longer than the days, with the thermometer dipping to an anesthetizing minus thirty-two degrees centigrade and the barrack's 320 inmates (all of them wearing their outdoor hoods indoors) looking on, Timur placed the palm of his hand where his heart would be under layers of clothing and swore to live by the *vory* code of honor or die trying. To seal the oath, he pricked the tip of his thumb with a whetted seal bone and smeared blood on his forehead. "*Na zdorovie*," Kosta exulted, raising his glass of iced rose-hip infusion to salute his protégé. "Welcome to our thieves' world."

"*Uraaa*, Timur the Lame!" Kosta's *vory* bellowed in chorus.

The principal activity in the Vorkuta tundra, apart from surviving the winter months, consisted of burrowing into the foothills of the Arctic's Ural Mountains to mine coal deposits. As a newly minted member of Kosta's *vory v zakone*, Timur was forbidden to join the thousands of prisoners working for the Communist regime in the mines. He wound up cutting the hair of *zeks* in the colony's barbershop—the only work permitted by the *vory* code because it gave him access to scissors and the device for sharpening them. (On the single rest day every month, he earned extra rations teaching teenage boys of political prisoners, who had been sent into exile with their parents, to pick pockets.) Armed with a pair of scissors and not being squeamish about using it, Timur quickly became one of Kosta's trusted enforcers. By the time the war ended in 1945, he had been elevated in rank to brigadier in charge of Kosta's gang of enforcers.

It was only at the death of the Great Helmsman, the Gardener of Human Happiness, the Master Architect of Communism, eight years after the end of the war, that the Soviet authorities got around to releasing ethnic prisoners from what was euphemistically called *preventive detention*. Summoned to the colony's administrative building, Timur managed to remain noncommittal when the Communist apparatchik, thinking he was doing him a favor, offered him a residence permit in Irkutsk on the Siberian shore of Lake Baikal. "Take it or leave it," he snapped in irritation, careful to keep a large table between himself and Kosta's enforcer. "Irkutsk is the only city where you are permitted to live *if* you leave Vorkuta." Taking the *if* as a threat, Timur's mentor, Kosta, counseled him to swallow his pride and pocket the damn residence permit before the apparatchik changed his mind. Timur took the old man's advice. Bidding Kosta a curiously emotionless farewell, he used the signed and sealed scrap of paper to stroll past the guards at the main gate, then, stowing it in his rucksack and turning his back on the penal colony, headed in the opposite direction from Irkutsk the moment he was out of sight of the perimeter watchtowers. In a journey that took the better part of eight months, he meandered across the Urals, stopping only to catch his breath in villages pretending to be towns or towns pretending to be cities before moving on, always and forever in the general direction of the horseshoe magnet of Moscow.

Once back in the capital, Timur moved into a small Ossete-run hotel across the street from the Soviet Ministry of Foreign Affairs that paid off the local constabulary to keep their noses out of its registry books. Careful to shave his three-day beard with a rusty razor in case he stumbled across a militiaman who might recognize the missing Vorkuta prisoner from mug shots circulating in police stations, Timur went into the business of providing carpenters or plumbers or electricians to ministry officials in return for blank passports. With the help of the Estonian sister who had survived the wartime bombardments and famine, he bartered forged passports for ration coupons, then made a killing selling ration coupons for rubles. Having served a twelve-year apprenticeship with Kosta Karatsev, Timur used the small fortune of cash he accumulated to recruit a band of Ossetes and form his own *vory v zakone*. They specialized in providing *krysha* to black-market retailers working out of illegal factories in Moscow's suburbs; for an honest 10 percent of the profits, Timur's *vory* collected debts, enforced contracts, discouraged competition, and kept less scrupulous gangs that charged a less-than-honest 20 percent for their services at arm's length.

By the late 1950s, Timur could afford to put a more respectable roof over his own head: He rented a suite of rooms on the top floor of the Oktyabrskaya Hotel. Originally built by the Central Committee of the Communist Party for its own use, the Oktyabrskaya boasted an elegant lobby with a marble stairway spiraling up to a marble bust of Lenin on the first-floor loggia, two bars that served imported Scotch whisky, and a glassed-in fitness club on the roof. Communist functionaries from around the world checked into the Oktyabrskaya when in Moscow, which opened new horizons for Timur's *vory v zakone*. He drew the line at supplying hard drugs, but a visiting Communist who required a Volga with or without a chauffeur, a woman or two for a night or two, a rendezvous with a particularly hard-to-pigeonhole commissar, or, harder still, two orchestra tickets to the Bolshoi could count on Timur and his *vory* friends—for a hefty fee paid in hard currency.

In 1965, Timur, much to his astonishment as he had never given the matter a second thought, fathered a boy by a young Ossete nurse with whom he felt a kinship that came uncomfortably close to an emotional attachment. Much to his regret, she didn't survive childbirth. Mourning his common-law wife, he refused to so much as set eyes on the boy, who was called Roman after the nurse's Italian father, a Communist who had come to Russia at the time of the Bolshevik Revolution to construct the new world order. Timur relented some weeks later when by chance he happened on a photograph of his son, taken when he was five minutes old, his eyes gaping open and staring with what can only be described as impatient curiosity at the world beyond the camera. If the death of Roman's mother broke Timur's heart, the look in the infant's eyes touched his heart. Determined to provide the boy with a home beyond a hotel room, he bought out (or frightened out) the tenants who lived in collective apartments in a tsarist banker's mansion on the Lenin Hills overlooking Moscow and began breaking down walls to restore the home to its prerevolutionary splendor.

He didn't get to live in the mansion for another ten years, the length of his second prison sentence after he was targeted in one of the Ministry of Internal Affairs' perennial anticorruption campaigns. Arrested for violating the catch-all Article 88 of the Soviet Criminal Code, branded a *socially dangerous element,* he was hauled before a special three-judge tribunal and, in a trial that lasted all of seven minutes, had a tenner pinned on him.

Which is how Timur ended up as the *pakhan* in Strict Regime Corrective Labor Colony No. 40, Kungur, Perm Region.

13
ROMAN:
TRYING TO DREAM HIS WAY OUT OF A NIGHTMARE . . .

Tuesday, January 14, 1992
Back to the frontstory

Roman, after several tries, succeeds in getting Yulia on her new satellite telephone the size of an American World War II lend-lease walkie-talkie. "I told you not to call me unless it was a matter of life or death," she tells him in an edgy whisper.

"It *is* a matter of life or death," he says. "I absolutely must talk to you."

"That's what you're doing."

"In person. Face to face."

"That's not possible. I am locked down. My father ordered me to remain in the hotel until the storm passed." She breathes into the phone. "I take sleeping pills but they don't help me sleep, for fuck's sake."

"Listen to me, Yulia, there's a spa on the third floor of the Narodnaya. I've been there once—"

"With a girlfriend?"

"I'm not a virgin, Yulia," he reminds her. "I was there with a girl who at the time was a friend. Listen, I know one of the girls who works in the spa; she's the daughter of the wife of one of our Ossetes. I can get in from the fire escape exit. They have dressing rooms—she'll tell me which one you're in. In an hour?"

"I'm not guaranteeing I can talk my way past Dad's guards in the hallway," she says. "I'll try. In an hour. If I'm not there, I'm not there."

Slipping into the spa from the fire door, Roman spots his contact, whose name is Osnat, at the far end of the corridor. She holds up five fingers. Roman waves his thanks, then lets himself into dressing room number five. He listens to the shower running in the bathroom for a moment, then pours himself a double shot of whiskey and downs half of it in one gulp. Behind him, Yulia emerges from the shower wrapped in a faded red bathrobe and drying her hair with a towel. Roman starts toward her but she holds up the palm of her hand like a traffic cop stopping a car, keeping him at arm's length. "I know what's happening, Roman," she whispers. "Our families are at war."

"That doesn't have to mean *we're* at war."

Padding barefoot to the buffet board, Yulia picks up Roman's half-filled glass of whiskey and sniffs at it. "Funny thing, I never liked the taste of whiskey but I always loved the smell," she says, talking to herself. She turns and, her voice logged with anger, talks to him. "I told you once: There is no us, Roman. There's a me, then there is a you. And this you—the you with Ossete blood in his veins and tales of Ossete bandits in his brain—this you was in the Porsche garage when one of my father's men got shot in the knee. Did you know the doctors at the clinic had to amputate his leg?"

"He was reaching for a pistol—"

"He was putting his hand in his pocket, for fuck's sake. Tell me you tried to stop your Argentine from exploding his kneecap!"

Yulia pulls the collar of her robe up around her neck and sinks onto a chair. "I can't imagine what I was thinking. Everyone knows that the Ossetes—even one who has been to London, where his rough edges ought to have been sanded off—are savages. Everyone knows there's a hair trigger on their brutishness."

Roman settles onto the floor, his back against a wall. "You are a prisoner of clichés."

Yulia's mouth falls open. "Jews have an intimate acquaintance with clichés. I am an Israelite, like my father, like my twin cousin, Tzuf, who is twelve minutes younger than me. If I should somehow happen to forget it, you can bet the world will remind me."

"The way you're reminding me I'm an Ossete, locked into the Ossete myth."

"Some mornings I wake up locked into the Jewish myth. Other mornings I wake up wishing I had never been born."

"Is that your spilt milk, Yulia? Wishing you'd never been born?"

"I'm damaged goods, Roman. I didn't need a finishing school—I needed a beginning school. I needed to start over again. That's my spilt milk." She tries to produce a teardrop and, thinking she has succeeded, brushes it away from the corner of her eye. "Go back to your Caucasus steppes, for God's sake. You'll be safer there. Here . . ."

"*Here* what?"

"Stay in Moscow, you'll end up shooting my kinsmen if your father orders you to. You could end up shooting me—"

"*Here* what?"

"Here you are in danger. Timur the Lame will surely retaliate for the Argentine. Caplan will retaliate for the retaliation. You and I are walking on a tightrope, Roman. Sure as hell, the both of us will end up victims of our fathers' lovely vicious circle."

"There's a way out, Yulia. Before we're locked into the circle, before we are killed by it, let's break out of jail. Tear sheets into strips, tie them together, scramble down the other side of the wall. What do you have to lose? Together. *Us.*"

"You're trying to dream your way out of a nightmare, Roman. You're trying to invent your life inside a fiction. Escape how? *How* escape?"

"Why are you damaged?"

"I've noticed that men make eye contact when they talk to me—ha, when they're not looking at my tits!—but women avoid my eye. Why do you think that is? Women are so much smarter than men. What do they see when they don't look me in the eye? What does contact with my eyes, or lack of same, tell someone about me?" Yulia slips a hand inside her robe, to her breast. "Escape how?"

"I have an English pal who has a small plane."

"My damage is my business. My spilt milk is my spilt milk."

"If you didn't want me to know, you wouldn't have told me about your spilt milk."

Tilting her head, smiling a smile that is not related to happiness, Yulia studies Roman. "I was never sure where you're coming from. I'm not sure where you're going. An Englishman. A plane. And?"

"Anthony fancies himself some sort of cartographer, but he is more of a rich playboy who taught himself to read aerial maps. He's been bumming around Europe in a vintage Cessna since he got his pilot's license. He could land, say, in the Bolshoye Gryzlovo Airfield, an hour from here by bus. If we could get there, he could fly us—*us!*—anywhere. Berlin. Rome. Paris. The French Riviera. A Greek island. Anywhere."

"You would have to support me in the style to which I want to become accustomed," she teased. "What would we do for money?"

"You could always get a job as a nude model."

"Do I have this right—in your scheme of things, I would wind up supporting you?"

"I was joking about the nude model. I could find work—"

"What skills do you have? Carpentry? Masonry? Electricity? Aside, it goes without saying, from your Ossete gangster skills like nicking the nose of bullets so they explode when they hit someone."

It dawns on Roman that Yulia is frightened out of her skin. "I could drive a taxi. A lot of White Russians wound up driving taxis in Paris after the Bolshevik Revolution." He pushes himself to his feet and pours himself another whiskey. "Want to sniff it?"

She tosses a shoulder in exasperation.

"Why are you damaged?"

"Could your English pal fly us to Yalta?"

"What's in Yalta?"

Yulia catches a distant glimmer of light at the end of her tunnel. "I have an aunt and uncle who manage the Livadiya Palace, the summer hidey-hole of Nicholas the Second, a long walk from Yalta. The palace is a museum that nobody visits, but there are apartments under the roof. My uncle and aunt live in one. They offered me bed and breakfast and tea and sympathy if I ever turned up on their doorstep."

"Yalta is not a half-bad idea. We could smuggle ourselves onto a ship heading for Greece through the Bosporus."

"I don't know."

"What don't you know?"

"Look, you have a lovely tattoo of angels on your chest, you're reasonably good in bed, I like you enough to fuck you, but I'm not sure I like you enough to fuck off with you." Yulia plucks an American filter-tip cigarette from a bowl on the table and, bending toward the flame on a candle, lights it.

Roman watches her watch the smoke spiral up from the tip of the cigarette. "I didn't know you smoked," he says.

"I don't. I used to. I stopped because I hate the smell of tobacco."

"Why did you smoke if you hate the smell of tobacco?"

"I like the taste. I like the gesture. I'm smoking now because I'm worried sick I'll be talked into accepting your proposition in the forlorn hope that it will put my demons to bed. When, as any idiot could figure out, running from them will only wake them up."

"You're . . . accepting?"

"What is it about *yes* that you can't get a grip on?" She sucks hard on her cigarette to keep the ember at the end lit. "I'm giving up smoking again as soon as I finish this one," she murmurs. "Don't celebrate—I'm thinking of becoming a pescetarian or, better still, a fruitarian. I'm planning to start drinking whiskey to wash down whatever I'm eating."

"I am celebrating," Roman shouts in a whisper. "Yalta, here we come!"

"Tell me something, Roman. Did your famous—or should I say *infamous*—father ever love someone?"

"He loves me."

"I mean a woman. Did he ever love someone other than himself?"

"I'm not sure he would have called it love. But yes, he felt an attachment—affection—for . . . someone."

"Who?"

"The woman who was my mother."

Yulia thinks about that. "I need to tell you, even when you smile you look sad. It's the eyes, Roman. Your eyes are a beautiful khaki, but the khaki turns muddy and ugly when you're sad. If you want to hide the sadness—from a woman, from me—you need to spend your waking hours with your eyes tight shut. It's called sleepwalking. The peasants say that sadness bends time. I've been told that happiness straightens time out, but I have no personal experience in the matter."

"Okay. Let's—let *us*!—straighten time out. Let's fly to Yalta and straighten time out."

"You are smiling that secret sad khaki smile of yours again."

"Am I?" He laughs. "I suppose I am."

14
RASPUTIN: SMELLING BLOOD, THE BEES COVER HIS EYELIDS, CLOG HIS NOSTRILS . . .

THE VILLAGE OF TZUKOI, DOWNRIVER FROM MOSCOW
Later on Tuesday

The messenger, sporting a leather helmet and goggles and a leather jacket worn back to front to turn it into a windbreaker, parks his fire-engine-red Voskhod motorcycle outside the gate of Timur's Lenin Hills mansion and hits the intercom button. "I got here a letter for somebody named Monsurov, Roman," he calls into the speaker box.

"Shove it through the mail slot," a voice instructs him.

"I need to have a signature," the messenger says.

"If you need a signature, sign the fucking thing and shove it through the slot and be quick about it." The messenger looks up at the security camera high on the stone wall. "Yeah, I'm watching you," the voice on the intercom warns. Shrugging, the messenger pushes the manila envelope through the slot, then climbs onto his Voskhod and, gunning the motor, heads downhill.

Inside the gate, one of the sixers retrieves the envelope. Gingerly holding it by an edge, he takes it down to the basement and passes it through Rasputin's brand-new x-ray device. "It's clean," the brigadier on watch announces. "Just paper inside." The sixer carries the envelope up two flights to Mikhail Rasputin, who is poring over the catalog of a Lebanese arms dealer specializing in surplus American military and police handguns. "Mika, you know where Roman is?" the sixer asks. "I have a letter for him."

"I'll take it," Rasputin says.

"It's addressed to Roman."

Rasputin looks up from the catalog to stare unblinkingly at the sixer. "Okay, yeah, sorry," the young man mutters, handing Mika the manila envelope.

Rasputin takes a nail file from a drawer and slits open the envelope. He pulls out a folded piece of typing paper and flattens it on the table. It is filled with large print written in capital letters. *ROMAN, YOU PIECE OF SHIT,* it begins. *IN THE TIME OF THE TSARS OUR GRANDFATHERS SETTLED THEIR LITTLE TRIBAL WARS IN A CIVILIZED WAY. THE SONS OF THE TWO FAMILIES MET IN A CODE DUELLO. I CHALLENGE YOU TO MEET ME ON THE SHELF ABOVE THE MOSCOW RIVER ACROSS FROM THE VILLAGE OF TZUKOI WHERE DUELS WERE FOUGHT FOR CENTURIES. ROW ACROSS THE RIVER AT DAWN TOMORROW. JUST THE TWO OF US ARMED WITH PISTOLS. ONLY ONE OF US WILL RETURN TO MOSCOW ALIVE. DO YOU HAVE THE BALLS TO ACCEPT? TZUF.*

The telephone ringing in the next room suddenly pierces Rasputin's eardrums. "Will someone answer the goddamn phone!" he calls. The ringing stops abruptly. A moment later Lice sticks his head into the room. "It's Roman," he tells Mika. "He wants to speak to you."

"Tell him I'm not here."

"I already told him you was here."

Mika, holding the letter in one hand, goes into the next room and plucks the phone off Lice's desk. "What's up, Roman?"

he demands. "When are you planning on leaving? . . . Your father won't be thrilled when I tell him what you're doing . . . How, not tell him? He will want to know where you are when you don't turn up for supper. What am I supposed to do, lie to him?" Mika listens for a long moment. "Lead your fucking life, then," he mutters. He glances at the letter in his hand. "No, nothing much going on here that you need to know about . . . I will. You too."

Hanging up the phone, Rasputin rereads Tzuf's letter, then folds it away in his pocket. He touches the four faded skulls tattooed on the backs of the fingers of his right hand. Lice, standing in the doorway, asks, "What are you smiling about, Mika?"

"I'm smiling about the fifth tattoo I'm going to add to my fingers."

"Who's the unlucky man?"

"Tzuf is the unlucky man. Listen up, Lice: Have my Range Rover ready to roll at four tomorrow morning. And you and Spare Rib with it."

"Armed?"

"I need you to turn up with the usual artillery. And two good binoculars."

"Where we off to, Mika?"

"We are going to picnic on the Moscow River."

Lice, who took Mika at his word, brings doughnuts and a thermos of hot coffee to the picnic. With the Range Rover parked alongside a barn on the southern edge of Tzukoi, Mika sips coffee in the thermos cap. The Moscow River, winding past the village below them, is clouded with a ribbon of mist that begins to burn off at first light, revealing a rowboat making its way through the silver ripples toward the ledge on the far shore. Focusing his binoculars on the rowboat, Rasputin can make out a man in an arctic parka with the hood over his head working the oars. There is a burst of static from the Motorola walkie-talkie. "You see him?" Rasputin asks Spare Rib, concealed on a rise crawling with blackberry brambles above the northern end of Tzukoi.

"He came in a Mercedes with three goons," Spare Rib, a bit breathless, reports. "They're still in the car. The motor's running—I can see exhaust. The guy rowing, he took one of the beached boats."

"Any sign of a rifle?" Rasputin demands.

"The rowboat was upside down on the pebbles when he righted it and pushed off, Mika. I could look down into it from where I'm at. There was a pair of rubber boots and a fishing rod under the seat but no rifle."

"You sure?"

"I'd bet my life on it."

"You're betting *my* life on it," Rasputin mutters to himself before flicking off the Motorola.

He raises his binoculars to examine the shelf of land across the river. It is fifteen or so meters wide and more or less the length of a soccer field. Nobody is visible on the shelf. Tucked under the overhanging cliff is a long row of wooden beehives of all shapes and sizes. Tzukoi, Rasputin remembers, is famous for its honey sold in the Fermerskiy Market. He fits on a pair of skintight leather gloves and, fetching one of the 9mm Belgium Parabellums from the satchel, unscrews the silencer. "Noise is not my problem," he tells Lice. "Accuracy is." He removes the thirteen-round magazine, then reinserts it with the heel of his hand and slips a second magazine into the pocket of his parka. "I hate to abandon the warmth of the car," he says cheerfully, "but I don't want to keep the prick waiting."

"Good hunting, Mika," Lice whispers.

"Why are you whispering?"

"I do not want to wake the dead."

"Or the soon-to-be dead," Rasputin says with a laugh.

On the sliver of beach below the village, Rasputin rights one of the upside-down boats and, pushing it into the water, clambers in and begins to row across the river. Beaching on the southern end of the shelf, he scrambles up the embankment and, shading his eyes with his hand, peers down the shelf at the far end. He spots the figure in the hooded parka making its way past the beehives toward him. Rasputin pulls the Parabellum from his pocket and, chambering a round, holds the pistol barrel down at his side. Squinting, he sees Tzuf hesitate—*Is he losing his nerve?*—and then flatten himself on the ground. *What is he up to*? Rasputin wonders. *If he shoots from that distance, he'll be wasting bullets.* A sickening suspicion forces its way into a lobe of his brain: *Tzuf was an army sniper in Afghanistan! Snipers are taught to shoot from a prone position. If he planted a sniper rifle on the shelf . . .*

A hollow shot reverberates through the wisps of mist rising from the river as a blunt-nosed bullet slams into Rasputin's kneecap. Flung backward onto his back, he doesn't feel pain, just the shock of the spike-maul jolt to his leg. He has the presence of mind to remember his Parabellum. *Need to find my pistol*, he thinks as the pain in his knee begins to seep into his consciousness. He bites hard on his tongue, tastes the blood seeping in his mouth. When he manages to open his eyes, he sees Tzuf standing over him, cradling a long Dragunov sniper rifle fitted with a telescopic sight in his arms. "Can you hear my voice?" Tzuf calls. "You're not Roman. Where the fuck is Roman? He was supposed to turn up here, not you." Rasputin, crazed with pain, wrenches the second magazine from his pocket and, thinking it is the pistol, tries to thumb one of the bullets at Tzuf, only to hear mocking laughter ringing in his ear.

Tzuf leans over his victim and spits words into his face. "The least you can do, considering all the trouble I went to to kill you, is come up with some memorable dying words, Mika Rasputin."

"Plague . . ."

"Plague?" Tzuf goads him. "What about a plague?"

"Plague on both—" Gagging on the bile in his throat, he is unable to finish the sentence.

Snickering, Tzuf picks up Rasputin's pistol and flings it into the river below the shelf. "You want a plague," he mutters. Fitting a beekeeper's thick canvas glove onto his right hand, he goes over to the hives under the overhang. Lifting the lid on one, he pulls a honeycomb crawling with bees from the hive and tosses it onto Rasputin's chest. "Here, I'll give you a plague," Tzuf sneers.

The bees, agitated, curdle on Rasputin's face, cover his eyelids, clog his nostrils and his ears. He lifts a hand to brush them away but the gesture is too feeble. A stifled scream escapes from his swollen lips as his mouth fills with angry bees.

15
ROMAN: I'M GOING TO SCRATCH MY VARIOUS LITTLE ITCHES . . .

MOSCOW

Wednesday, January 15, 1992

Lice is fighting back tears. "I watched the whole fuckin' thing through binoculars from across the river. I did not know what to do, Roman. I could see Tzuf looking at me through his telescopic sight. I needed to duck behind the car real quick. He had three goons waiting for him in the Mercedes. Spare Rib was somewhere on the other side of the village. There was nothing—"

Roman nods. "I'm not blaming you."

"When they was gone, Spare Rib and me, we rowed across the river. Bees or no bees, we would have collected poor Rasputin's corpse, but we heard police sirens so we got us the hell outa there. Christ, you did not want to see his face—it was bloated up from the stinging. He did not look nothin' like our Mika no more. What a way to get murdered . . ." He produces a letter from his pocket. "Mika had this on him. It was addressed to you but it was delivered to him."

Roman, reading Tzuf's letter—*ROMAN, YOU PIECE OF SHIT*—is

reminded of Ophelia quoting Hegel in Barcelona: *Seen from shoe level, history is a* Schlachtbank*—a slaughterhouse.*

"Tell me what do we do?" Lice pleads. "Tell me where do we do it?"

"I need to speak to my father," Roman says. He thinks he is talking to himself and is startled at the high-pitched sound of his own voice in his ear. "My father," he thinks out loud, "will know what to do."

In the stairwell, Roman overhears his father's end of a phone conversation. Timur, trying to control his temper, is speaking in glacial tones to someone at the morgue about releasing Rasputin's body for burial. Suddenly, talking to Yulia seems more important to Roman than talking to his father. Retreating to his bedroom on the third floor, locking the door behind him, he sits on the edge of the bed and punches in the number of Yulia's satellite phone. He presses the phone to his ear and listens as it rings a dozen, fifteen times. He is on the verge of giving up when Yulia comes on the line. "It's me," he says. "Something happened. We need to talk."

"Damn right something happened. You're the last person I want to talk to," she says. "I need to stay away from you and your peacock phrases. My father . . ."

"My father too," he says when she doesn't finish the sentence.

"You're going to murder my kid cousin Tzuf, aren't you?"

"If I can, I will. He murdered my best friend, Rasputin."

"It was a fair fight, a duel . . ."

"Where do you get your information?"

"Where do you get *your* information?"

"From an eyewitness," Roman tells her. "There was nothing fair about it, Yulia. Your kid cousin Tzuf killed Rasputin with bees."

"How can you kill someone with bees, for fuck's sake?"

"Tzuf wasn't gunning for Rasputin, he was out to kill me. Rasputin intercepted his letter—"

"What letter?"

"Rasputin was stung to death, Yulia."

"Whatever happened to the us you hoped for, Roman?"

"Meet me, Yulia."

She hesitates. "Where? When?"

He gives her an address of a coffee shop in a small hotel that just opened on a side street off the Arbat. "At ten tonight."

"I don't know," she says.

"What don't you know?"

"I don't know if the angel tattooed on your chest can protect the flame." For a moment the line seems to go dead. Yulia's voice mixed with a burst of static comes back on. ". . . you hate me?"

"Yes . . . No. There are moments when I think I love you and moments when I . . ."

"Finish the goddamn sentence, for fuck's sake. When you?"

"When I wish I'd never set eyes on you ice-skating."

"What are you going to do about Tzuf?"

Roman listens to the sound of Yulia breathing into the phone. "To use Dostoyevsky's lovely phrase about our 'various little itches,' I'm going to scratch mine," he murmurs, then cuts the connection.

Making his way to the fourth floor, Roman sees his father and a *vor* he doesn't recognize leaning over an architectural plan spread out on the table. Timur looks up. "You don't know Spider," he tells his son. "He's from the Muslim village next to my grandfather's. The Black Sea Marines trained him in the delicate art of fabricating bombs. Say hello to my son, Roman, Spider."

Spider, a dark Ossete with the tight facial skin of an onion and a faded tattoo of a sputtering fuse under an eye, nods once. Roman asks him, "So who are you going to blow up?"

"Whoever your father decides needs blowing up."

Timur's bad nostril whistles as he tells his son, "Spider here is what the Muslims call a *hafiz*—a guardian of the Qur'an who can recite all hundred fourteen suras by heart. Go ahead, test him—name a sura, Roman."

"One hundred fourteen."

Spider's eyes narrow into a sightless squint; his fingers toy with the gold ring in the lobe of his left ear. "Sura one hundred fourteen: *Bismi-llāhi r-raḥmāni r-raḥīm*. I seek refuge in Allah, the Lord of mankind, the King of mankind, the Judge of mankind, from the evil of the whisperer—"

Roman interrupts. "Identify the whisperer."

Spider looks from the son to the father and back to the son. "It is well understood the devil is the whisperer."

"And what did the devil whisper?" Roman persists.

Spider glances uncertainly at Timur, who wags a finger. "Instruct my son," he orders the new Ossete bomb maker.

"The devil whispered into the ear of the Jew Lobeid," Spider says, "to tie eleven knots in a cord to bewitch the Prophet, of sacred name. The commentators teach us that the archangel Jibreel told the Prophet where the cord was hidden. The Prophet sent his son-in-law Ali to fetch the cord. Reciting verses of the Holy Qur'an, at every verse the Prophet loosed a knot until the cord was free of knots and the Prophet was free of the curse."

Timur says pointedly, "I remember the grandmother of my father, who was blessed with the wisdom that comes with age—she passed at a hundred and one—identifying a man and a woman in Areshperani who had 'tied the knot.' When I worked up the nerve to ask her what she meant, she explained that they were bewitched by love. Beware of tying knots with Jewesses, my darling son."

Roman looks Timur in the eye. "I could never quite figure out whether you were anti-Semitic or merely anti-Caplan, my father."

"To respond to your disrespectful, not to mention tactless, remark"—Spider turns away in embarrassment to study the laces on his shoes—"I make no secret of my disesteem for Israelites. I combat Caplan not because he is Israelite but because he is stepping on my toes and, in the process, staining your father's reputation. Which is why you, out of loyalty to your father and allegiance to his Ossete *vory*, need to loosen the knots with his niece, Rosalyn, and his daughter, Yulia."

"A son's love for his father is also a knot," Roman can't resist remarking. Taking a certain satisfaction in the discomfort on his father's face, he turns back toward the door.

"I didn't give you leave to leave," Timur barks.

"I need air."

"We don't lack for air in this room."

"I need *fresh* air, Father."

Once outside the mansion, Roman starts walking uphill along a one-lane road that meanders between prerevolution villas set in tangled, unkempt gardens. He is trying to put his father's obsession with knots and Lice's description of Rasputin's bee-stung face out of his head when a black American Packard pulls up ahead, blocking the lane. The rear door opens and a man sticks his head out. "Remember me, Roman Timurovich?" he calls.

Gripping the revolver in the pocket of his parka, Roman is careful to keep his distance from the car. "No."

"You audited my course on the Italian mafia a lifetime ago."

Roman puts a name to the face. "Axelrod. Osip Axelrod. You

claimed the only difference between the Italian mafia and the Russian mafia was language—one spoke Italian, the other Russian."

"I wasn't wrong."

"Your explanation was too simplistic. That's a nice car you have. What do you do for a living these days?"

"I'm a cop. I work for the Sixth Bureau of the Organized Crime Control Department."

"Figures. You work out of the MVD building that should have been twenty floors but wound up circumcised."

Axelrod grins. "Ha! I have to remember that. From now on, when someone asks me where I work, I'll tell them in a circumcised building."

"I don't talk to cops when I can help it."

"You need to talk to me. I want to do you a favor."

Roman takes a step toward the Packard. He notices the driver watching him in the wing mirror. "Tell your guy to put both his hands on the wheel," he says.

Axelrod laughs. The driver laughs with him as he raises both his hands to grip the wheel. "You're right to be jumpy," Axelrod says. "Caplan's nephew, Tzuf, is gunning for you. He killed your pal Rasputin thinking he was killing you."

"How would you know this?"

"Ever heard of wiretaps?"

"What's the favor you want to do for me?"

"We have Tzuf coming to our circumcised building for questioning at four this afternoon. Needless to say, he will have an ironclad alibi—a dozen people who will swear on a stack of Bibles, or Marx's *Das Kapital*, that he was at a breakfast party, three girls who will swear they were in bed with him, whichever. We're planning to keep him talking about his alibi for an hour and fifteen minutes. At five fifteen, when it begins to get dark outside, we will reluctantly inform him that he is free to go and take him down the back staircase to a small side door on Sredniy Karetnyy, across from the Zhukov statue. We'll keep his phone so he won't be able to call a taxi. He'll have to walk past Zhukov on his way to the metro."

Roman steps still closer. "Why are you telling me this?"

"My director is a firm believer that the solution to our *vory v zakone* problem in Moscow is to let you people kill each other off. The more bodies there are, the more work there is for the undertaker and the less work there is for us." Axelrod reaches for the shoebox at his feet. He offers it to Roman. "Present to you from your professor who thinks the only difference between the Italian mafia and our homegrown Russian *vory* is language."

"What is it?"

"The latest toy from America. It won't bite. Take it."

Roman opens the shoebox. Inside is a beautiful .357 Magnum Colt with a silencer screwed onto the barrel and what looks like a long, thin flashlight fastened on top. He flicks on the flashlight's switch. A needle of yellow light dances on the sidewalk at his feet. "A laser gunsight!" Roman murmurs. He remembers the late and much-lamented Rasputin taking him into a field to practice shooting a Parabellum and telling him about the existence of laser sights on pistols. This is the first time he has set eyes on one. He glances curiously at Axelrod. "Why?"

The chief of the Sixth Bureau permits a knowing smile onto his lips. "Why not?" He laughs under his breath at a private joke as he pulls the car door closed and taps the driver on the shoulder. The Packard purrs to life and moves slowly off up the narrow street.

It crosses Roman's mind that he is being set up—Axelrod's Sixth Bureau could be hoping to kill two birds with one scheme—so he is careful to show up two hours before dusk and, fitting himself into Zhukov's shadow, listens to Lice, watching through binoculars from a nearby hotel roof, on his earbud as he describes everyone within a stone's throw of the small park. "White male, twenty-something, aviator sunglasses, civilian clothing but paratrooper lace-up boots and cap, crossing to your right. Three old men with paper hats folded from *Pravda*, I can read the fucking headlines with my binoculars, walking single file along the narrow dirt path behind you—they look like they're performing on a tightrope. White male, fifty-something, pince-nez pinching his ski-jump Israelite nose, civilian clothing, coming from the metro side. Not-so-white male panhandling on the side street off the park."

After a while, as the end-of-afternoon iciness starts to bite, pedestrian traffic thins out.

A soot-thick darkness, mixed with a fine rain that could turn to sleet if the drops grow bigger, begins to saturate the city. Suddenly, a crackle of static fills Roman's earbud. "Oh, Jesus on the cross, it is fucking *him*," Lice cries excitedly. "He came out the side door of the GRU cheesecake."

"You're positive about the ID?" Roman whispers into his lapel pin.

"It is him, all right, no hat, wiping rain off his forehead with the back of his sleeve."

Tzuf, passing the Zhukov statue in the thickening dusk, hears someone call his name as he notices the yellow insect dancing on his chest.

He never hears the muffled cough of the Colt.

"You did good, my son," Timur tells Roman. Peering into his eyes, struck by the absence of emotion in them, he racks his brain for something comforting to say. "It is never easy to kill someone," is the best he can come up with.

"You are speaking from experience, my father?"

"I am. I am." He sits down alongside Roman and puts a hand on his knee. "Are you all right?"

"No."

"With time—"

"I enjoyed it."

"Pardon?"

"I enjoyed killing him, my father. My fingertips tingled. I'm not sure but I may have even gotten an erection. Killing him gave me pleasure."

Timur accepts this with a nod. "There's nothing out of the ordinary in taking pleasure from revenging a close friend," he says. "This Tzuf had it coming. He didn't give Mika a chance on the ledge."

"I don't want to be this person who enjoys killing someone."

"What's really troubling you is not the killing of Tzuf. What bothers you is discovering something about yourself that you didn't know and don't particularly like. It's a Styx I crossed a lifetime ago, my son."

"And how did you cope, my father?"

Timur shrugs. "Like an allergy, you learn to live with it."

Roman sits down next to Yulia in the booth of the small backstreet hotel coffee shop off the Arbat.

"I killed your kinsman."

"Tzuf?"

"Tzuf."

Yulia looks away, clearly distracted. But by what? The death of Tzuf? Her failure to take it as hard as she thought she should? The terrible reality that it was her most recent one-night stand who killed him? All of the above? "Identify the thing you like most about me," she demands, counting on a new subject to make the old one go away.

"Did you hear what I said, Yulia?" He edges closer to her on the banquette and offers her a new subject to hang around her neck. "The thing I like most about you is you look as good without clothes as with."

"Seriously. I need you to name the thing."

"The thing I like most about you is you still cry over spilt milk."

The old subject rears its ugly head. "I'm not stupid, Roman," she snaps. "I know you killed Tzuf, for God's sake. I know my kid cousin killed your friend whose name I can't remember—"

"Rasputin."

"Rasputin. Is that a code name? You people have code names, don't you?" She doesn't leave space between her questions for an answer but rambles on, adrift in her own narrative. "Tzuf killed your friend with bees. I overheard one of my father's *vory* who was there, who watched from across the river. I heard him describe the hives and the bees and the end of the world I thought I knew. The Tzuf who could do that is not the Tzuf who introduced me to the male genital." She chews on her lower lip. "He's not the kid cousin I looked up to since we were kids. Oh fuck," she mutters. "As if I didn't have enough spilt milk in my life."

"Two of our people wind up dead and you're feeling sorry for yourself. This is not about you."

"You expect me to rend my clothes and go into mourning? Fuck that. I don't do mourning, Roman from another planet." She glances at the hand-lettered sign over the bar that declares *The Customer Is the Enemy*; she looks at the three tourists sitting at the table just inside the door to the street—Englishmen, from the look of their furry sideburns and the empty beer bottles lined up on the serving tray as if they're keeping score. "It is about me, Roman. I thought being a fruitarian would solve my problem. It didn't. I need to escape from this thieves' world of my father and your father. I need to find another world to live in."

"I'm sorry the fruitarian thing didn't work out for you." Roman takes several nervous breaths, working up the courage to articulate the words trapped on the tip of his tongue. "Me also, I need to find another world to live in," he finally manages to blurt out. He touches her fingers, which are drumming nervously on the table. "How about if we look for another world together."

"How about," she agrees.

"You haven't changed your mind?"

Yulia laughs wildly. The Englishmen near the door glance in her direction. "What is it about *yes* that you can't get a handle on?" she demands.

"I was terrified you might be having second thoughts about Yalta," Roman explains lamely. "I've spent most of my life sleepwalking in my father's shadow. I'd more or less abandoned hope of waking up."

He's not sure she has heard him or, if she has, whether what he said has registered. "Goes to show how desperate a girl can be, clutching at straws in the blizzard," she murmurs with a catch in her voice that betrays the teardrop she is blinking away in the corner of her eye. "Where did you get that shirt? London?"

"No. It's East German."

"Nobody wears East German shirts if they can help it."

"East Germans wear East German shirts." He starts to say something, then swallows the words before they can pass his lips.

"Say it," Yulia orders.

"I was going to say that it all boils down to who you trust," he says, thinking out loud.

"No, no, you are a prisoner of your maleness. It's not who you trust, it's who you love."

He shakes his head once. "I love my father, but I'm not sure I trust him."

She thinks about this. "I love my father too . . ." She shakes her head violently, unable to finish the thought.

"I trust you," he whispers.

"Fuck you."

He laughs. "Fuck me," he agrees.

Sighing, she consults Wednesday's specials, chalked onto a blackboard set on an easel. She consults the rings on both her thumbs. Roman has the queasy feeling she would have consulted her navel if she hadn't been wearing a Chinese army quilted jacket over a cashmere jumper over a flannel shirt buttoned up to her very pale neck.

16
ROMAN AND YULIA: A FEW WEEKS AGO I WAS OLDER THAN I AM NOW . . .

LIVADIYA PALACE, NEAR YALTA

Thursday, January 16, 1992

"Does she speak English?" Anthony asks Roman, who is sitting in the Cessna's copilot's seat.

"I never asked her."

"Ask, ask."

Roman turns in his seat. "*Ty govorish po-anglijski?*" he asks Yulia, who is staring out the scratched window behind the pilot, mesmerized by the sight of the Volga, which Anthony is following as he flies over the Nizhny Novgorod Kremlin and, banking southwest, heads for the Crimea and the Simferopol airport some sixty kilometers from Yalta.

"English!" she says. "I wish."

"She doesn't."

"Pity. I could have had a conversation with her. She's got bloody nice knees, Roman. Where did you excavate her?"

"Ice-skating in Gorky Park. She wore black tights and a short red skirt."

"What are you telling him?" Yulia shouts to be heard over the propeller.

"I was describing the first time I set eyes on you ice-skating on the Gorky pond."

Yulia turns back to the window. "I don't like being in an aeroplane," she shouts.

"Why?"

Her cat eyes narrow into slits and flit from side to side as if they fear to focus on any one thing. "I worry they're too heavy to get off the ground. I worry they're too heavy to stay in the air if they do get off the ground." She slams one heel of an ankle-length boot into the floorboard. "There's nothing under us but theory, Roman, for God's sake."

"I get it—you're afraid of dying?"

"You're not?"

"I'm afraid of suffering. I'm afraid of becoming a vegetable. I'm afraid of living what's left of my life without you."

"Fuck you."

It has become a code of intimacy between them. "Fuck me," he agrees.

For the first time since he has used his trusty rejoinder on her, she doesn't suppress a grin, which almost qualifies as a genuine smile.

Anthony, humming an aria from *Traviata* under his breath, from time to time singing a few words in something resembling Italian, plunges the Cessna into a towering cumulus. The plane shudders. A thermos falls from an overhead compartment and rolls along the deck until Roman leans back and secures it. "The bloke who taught me how to fly claimed that cumulus clouds scrubbed the skin of the plane clean," Anthony shouts, giggling with pleasure. As the Cessna breaks out of the cloud, the Volga, with its ice floes and riverside villages lost in endless birch forests, unfurls off to port. A thousand meters below the Cessna, a speck of a biplane can be seen dusting fields of winter wheat with plumes of white spray that are larger than the biplane's wingspan. Anthony shouts, "Another half hour should see us home."

Yulia turns back from her reflection in the oval window. "We made love once, Roman," she shouts. "Do you remember every detail? Do you—*can* you—relive it in that befuddled brain of yours?"

"We made love twice, once at night, again the next morning," he shouts.

"Oral sex doesn't count."

Anthony, catching bits and pieces of the conversation, pushes one of the earphones away from his ear. "What is *oralny seks*?" The penny drops. "Ah, I get it," he shouts. Fabricating a pistol out of his thumb and forefinger, he aims at Roman and pulls the trigger twice. "Jammy Russian bastard!"

Roman mimes being shot, then, laughing, twists in his seat and yells back to Yulia, "I remember it all—every gesture, every moment, every imperfection of your body."

"Identify an imperfection!"

"Your ears are too big, your navel is filled with lint—"

Yulia cuts him off. "You have actually explored my navel?"

"There is no nook or cranny of you that I haven't explored. I'm not finished with your imperfections. Your lips—all of them—are chapped, the nipple on your right breast points in a different direction than your left breast, the sea green of your eyes reminds me of the ocean after a storm, not before."

She thinks about this. "*If* we were to become an us, Roman—I'm not saying it's a done deal—*if* we were to grow old together for, say, forty years and if during those forty years we made love twice a week, which is a hundred times a year, we would have fucked four thousand times. So my question is, would you remember each of the four thousand times we made love?"

"What about four thousand times?" Anthony yells when Roman translates the number but not the sentence.

"Absolutely," Roman shouts back to Yulia. "I would memorize every single time the way I memorized the first two, I swear it."

"The first time was one, Roman, not two." Yulia swallows a smile. "So, you're lying through your teeth about the four thousand, but I'm beginning to like more than the naked angel tattooed on your chest."

"Like? Not love?"

"Like has a longer shelf life than love."

"Says who?"

"Me, goddamn it," Yulia shouts. "Says me is who."

Anthony's two passengers pass an anxious moment when they discover that their pilot is unable to contact the control tower at Simferopol airport. When someone finally replies, she speaks English with a Russian accent so strong Anthony doesn't understand a word she says. Roman saves the day. He asks the controller to repeat in Russian and translates. "Roger, wind west at seven knots on runway W2," he tells the air traffic controller.

"Honestly?" Yulia shouts. "All four thousand?"

The air traffic controller's static-filled voice fills the cockpit. "Simferopol to Cessna: You are on a flight path that will take you over a military air base"—sure enough, Roman can make out silver cigar-shaped jets parked in revetments up ahead—"which, like cigarette smoking, can be dangerous for your health, as they don't take kindly to overflights. Seriously urge you to detour around."

"Detouring around," Anthony shouts when Roman relays the warning.

"*Idyom v obhod*," Roman repeats into Anthony's microphone.

Aside from a bit of skidding on the ice-slick runway, Anthony manages to touch down his Cessna in a textbook-perfect three-point landing, which leaves him giggling as he powers up to a hangar filled with fuel trucks. "I am chuffed—can't get much better than that," he announces, congratulating himself and relishing the praise. "On commercial flights passengers break into applause when the pilot brings the plane in."

"They applaud," Yulia explains when Roman translates, "because they're relieved to still be alive."

Anthony cuts the motor, then nudges Roman in the ribs to draw his attention to the young woman in tight jeans putting wooden chocks under the Cessna's wheels. "When's the last time you saw an ass like that?" he stage-whispers.

Yulia, unbuckling the seat belt digging into her breast, catches the meaning from Anthony's leering tone. "I thought he was homosexual," she tells Roman.

"I'm that too," Anthony says with a giggle when Roman translates.

"So where you people off to?" asks the grandmother driving the airport's dilapidated black taxi, a vintage Zil that has almost eight hundred thousand kilometers on the odometer and sounds more like a tank than a passenger car.

"Livadiya Palace," Roman tells her.

"Livadiya Palace! Took two Americans there summer before last summer. They turned straight round and raced back to Yalta when they went and discovered it didn't got no golf course. You folks looking for a golf course, you're barking up the wrong palace."

"Could you talk less and drive more slowly?" Yulia demands from the back seat.

"I can sure talk less," the grandmother mutters, "but it's me who gets to decide what speed to drive at. You don't like how I drive, you need to find yourselves another taxi."

"Is there another taxi at Simferopol?"

"Not since 1982."

Anthony whistles in admiration when he catches sight of the Livadiya Palace sprawling behind manicured hedges. "Bloody hell!" he exclaims. "I guess that's what Russia must have been like before the Communists stunted its growth."

Yulia's uncle Olezka, a brother of Naum Caplan's first wife, Yulia's mother, is sitting at an enormous marble table in the vast entrance, a small electric heater aimed at his feet, its coils glowing red, his old borzoi bitch sprawled like a sheepskin in front of the great chimney filled with the ashes of the palace's wooden fences, which were uprooted and burned when firewood became too expensive. Crumbs of cake and a thermos of tea are on a week-old copy of *Pravda* spread across the table like a cloth. Uncle Olezka is wearing rumpled corduroy trousers tucked into his scuffed gum boots and a washed-out Don Cossack cavalry officer's tunic, its frayed collar turned up around his wrinkled neck, a single medal pinned over the breast pocket—the silver Partisan of the Patriotic War with its profile of Stalin and Lenin. "Yulia, dear girl," he cries when he catches sight of his niece coming through the sumptuous double doors.

She rushes over to plant moist kisses on his unshaven cheeks. "Uncle Olezka, you said you could put me up in one of your attic rooms if I ever came back. Does the offer still stand?"

"Dear girl, of course it still stands. You are a sight for my very sore eyes."

"And where is Auntie Aksinia?"

Olezka scratches in discomfiture at the scraggly fluff of lint on his chin that passes for a beard. "She passed a year and a half and two weeks ago, my dear. They told me it was lung cancer. I told them it couldn't be lung cancer as Aksinia never smoked a cigarette in her life. Water under the bridge, as the peasants say." He lifts one reedy shoulder in a shrug logged with resignation. "We were happy here, living in the anus of the ancient regime, as it were." He glances over his shoulder at the portrait on the wall behind him of the dowager empress Maria Feodorovna, who fled Russia from Livadiya after the Bolshevik Revolution on a British warship sent by her nephew George V. "Livadiya was our Varykino," Olezka tells Yulia, "the Ural estate where the doctor Zhivago and his Lara tried to hide from the world in Pasternak's fairy—or should I say terror—tale."

Yulia turns to Roman. "It shall be our Varykino also."

Anthony is craning his neck to take in the enormous stained-glass oval skylight above the entranceway. "Being here is the closest thing to time travel, to going back to a previous century."

Roman keeps his eyes on Yulia as he talks to Anthony. "I don't believe in time travel," he tells him. "If it were possible, people from the future would be turning up on our doorstep."

"Maybe they have," Anthony offers with a sly wink. "Maybe we didn't recognize them."

Uncle Olezka, sizing up Anthony, asks Yulia, "Who's the fat fellow?"

"Our pilot, Anthony," Yulia explains. "We flew from Moscow in his aeroplane. The other one is my lover and"—she is startled by the words on the tip of her tongue before she hears herself pronounce them—"and my love. His name is Roman." She quickly adds, as if making a joke will pull the sting, "Roman is, thanks to God, Russian. Anthony is, through no fault of his, English."

"Ah yes, English, is he? I might have guessed." Uncle Olezka smiles the tight-lipped smile people perfect to hide bad teeth. "The Brits starved half to death from 1940 to '45, then started stuffing themselves with mutton and never stopped."

"I say, is he talking about me?" Anthony inquires.

"He's talking about the war," Roman tells him.

"Which one?" Anthony demands. He snickers. "Being Russian, perhaps he has lost count."

Yulia stretches a bare arm from the narrow, stone-hard bed to snare several Tashkent grapes that Uncle Olezka has left in a dish on the night table. She listens for a long moment to Roman's steady breathing before edging out from under the heavy quilted blanket to make her way on bare feet to the only window in the low-ceilinged attic room. Unhooking the knob, she pulls it open, then reaches over the wads of cotton spread on the sill to unlock the outer storm window.

A gust of biting sea air shrieks through the room. Roman, alarmed, props himself up on one elbow. "What the hell are you doing?" he demands in an urgent whisper.

"I'm letting the outside in."

"It must be ten below, Yulia!" As his eyes become accustomed to the darkness, he can make out the long shadow of her bare back across the room. "Why in God's name would you plant yourself stark naked in front of an open window?"

"To smell the sea. I know it's out there, smothered in frost and fog. When I was a girl in Vilnius, I spent several vacations in Klaipeda on the coast with a beautiful woman who told me she was a motion-picture actress. I was instructed to call her Aunt Esther, but as neither of my parents had a sister, with hindsight I think she must have been my father's mistress. When Aunt Esther was napping, I would sneak up to the attic and open a small window to get a whiff of the Baltic."

"Even in winter?"

"Especially in winter," she says with a soft laugh. "In summer it often smells of sewage. In winter it smells of hoarfrost; its saltiness stings your nostrils."

"There are parts of you I haven't explored yet," Roman murmurs. "Come back under the blanket before you freeze to death."

"Come see, the lights of Yalta are tinting the underbelly of the clouds yellow."

"No thank you."

With a laugh, Yulia fastens shut the outer storm window and the inner window. She draws a heart on the moist glass with a fingertip and pierces it with a long arrow. Padding silently across the wide floorboards to the narrow bed, she slips back into Roman's arms. He shivers. "You're icy," he remarks. "But even icy, you warm me."

After a while Yulia says, "When we lived in Vilnius, I had a cat. I called her Tunnel because she was as black as a tunnel with no glimmer of light at the end. My Tunnel used to sit on my window ledge for hours watching the birds. And one day . . ."

"One day," he prompts when she hesitates.

"One day a bird flew too close to the ledge and her instincts kicked in and my darling Tunnel leaped at the bird. We were seven floors up. I collected her warm broken body in a brown paper bag and buried her in the garden behind our building."

"Is that what you were doing at the window? Waiting for some poor bird to fly by so you could leap after it?"

She reaches down with two fingers to touch his penis, which is soft and warm and, curiously, reminds her of the dead Tunnel. "You are my bird, Roman."

"You wouldn't have said that a few weeks ago."

"A few weeks ago I was older than I am now. With you, I seem to be growing younger by the day."

"Younger?"

"Younger, as in permitting myself to hope." After a moment she adds in a husky voice, "You do see it, Roman—we are trapped in a tunnel, you and I. If we are lucky enough to reach the end, do you think we will discover light?"

"It is a law of nature," he tells her; he tells himself. "Where the tunnel ends, light begins."

17
SPIDER:
I RIGGED THE FIREWORKS NOT TO START UNTIL THE ENGINE HEATS UP FROM DRIVING . . .

MOSCOW

Friday, January 17, 1992

Spare Rib, behind the wheel of the late lamented Rasputin's trusty Range Rover, turns into a bleak Moscow suburb and double-parks in front of the Smirnoff distillery, the last stop on the monthly round collecting envelopes filled with cash from Timur's roofs. "I'll hold the fort," he tells Timur's two enforcers, Lice and Spider, the Ossetes' new bomb maker.

"How come you get to hold the fort in the heated car?" Lice complains.

Spare Rib says, "Look, I did the hard-currency store and the Jap restaurant on Gorky. Now it's your turn. Okay?"

"Being not okay won't change nothing," Lice mutters with a cantankerous shake of his head.

The two enforcers, each with one hand on the revolver in the deep pocket of his duffle coat, Spider chain-smoking Belomorkanals, make their way through the front door of the distillery and start down the dark, narrow passage leading to a warren of well-lit offices. Passing through the outer office, Lice, his nicotine-stained fingers scratching at a long sideburn, notices that the three secretaries, typing away on newfangled computer keyboards, don't look up from their screens. "So where was you ladies raised?" he scolds the women. "How much would it cost you to wish us good morning?"

The youngest secretary, with a silver streak in her dyed red hair, lifts her eyes from the computer screen. "Sure, why not? Good morning to you mafia gentlemen come to collect your monthly pocket money," she says with a saucy lilt to her voice.

"Fuck you, Baba Yaga," Lice snaps.

"Hey, if I really was the famous witch," the secretary shoots back brazenly, "you can bet a fat loser like you would never make it past the magical gate I fabricated out of my victims' bones!"

The other secretaries smother their laughter. Bristling at the girl's impudence, Lice takes a step in her direction. Spider plucks at Lice's duffle coat. "We got other birds to kill," he mutters. He turns and raps a knuckle twice on the opaque glass window of the inner office, then pushes open the door with the toe of his lace-up boot.

Lice, one step behind Spider, tightens his grip on the revolver when he spots the man sitting on one of the room's radiators. "I know you," Lice snarls. "I know him," he tells Spider. "His name is Axelrod, he is one of the jokers in the Sixth Bureau of the Organized Crime Control crowd."

"I'm not *one* of the jokers," Axelrod says with a cold smile. "I'm the *chief* joker." He raises both hands so the two enforcers can see them. "I am armed—with useful information for your bomb maker here."

"Why would the likes of you be giving me useful information?" Spider demands.

Axelrod takes in the faded tattoo of a sputtering fuse under

Spider's right eye, the gold ring gleaming in the lobe of his left ear. "So you can light the fuse at a time and in a place that will give satisfaction to my director, who is convinced the solution to our *vory v zakone* problem is to let you fellas knock each other off."

"We are here to collect the monthly fee for protecting the distillery," Lice says. "Your so-called information does not interest us."

"When you hear my information, you'll think it is more valuable than the envelope stuffed with rubles on the desk over there."

Retrieving the envelope, Lice flicks through the bills with a thumb, checking their denomination, then nods at Spider to indicate the monthly payment looks right. He glances at Axelrod, who still has both palms in the air. "You can put your paws down," Lice says. "Okay, spit it out. What is this valuable information you are flogging?"

"Naum Caplan occupies the two top floors of a hotel in the Jewish Quarter. He parks his vehicles on the first level of the hotel's subbasement garage."

"You are not telling us nothing we do not already know," Lice says. "Caplan has got hisself three Mercedes, three BMWs, one Saab, plus the two armored Studebakers from the Great Patriotic War, one of which actually runs, the other of which is jacked up and is waiting for the god of spare parts to deliver a new Studebaker carburetor."

Clapping his hands in mock applause, Axelrod slips off the radiator. "You forgot the baby-blue Porsche 911 Turbo three-point-three-liter—"

"That there is his daughter's toy," Lice says with a sneer. "I see where you are going, Comrade Chief of the Sixth Bureau. You can bet your last ruble we already cased the garage. The staircase from the hotel lobby is a dead end, the doors have been welded shut on every level of the subbasement, which leaves the elevator, for which you need a passkey. Even if you was to somehow get your paws on the passkey, even if the guy in the hotel's security room turned out to be fast asleep instead of keeping his eyes glued to the screens, you got watchmen and a Doberman patrolling the subbasements twenty-four on twenty-four."

"My compliments. I see you have done your homework. But you omitted an intriguing detail. The two watchmen keeping an eye on Caplan's cars during the night—they are former Sixth Bureau cops who work for me. At seven sharp tonight the fire door that is locked and chained shut on the inside will be open for one hour. The fire door gives out onto a corkscrew metal staircase that ends in the alleyway used by the hotel's laundry service."

Lice and Spider exchange looks.

Spider exhales thin plumes of Belomorkanal smoke from his nostrils. "How can we be sure you are not feeding us to the crocodiles?" he demands.

"Easy. Climb down the corkscrew staircase and try the fire door," Axelrod suggests. "If it doesn't open, you can always lodge a complaint with the Sixth Bureau the next time our paths cross. Assuming there will be a next time."

Timur the Lame finishes the last of his beetroot soup and, pushing the bowl away, bends closer to the edge of the tablecloth to wipe his mouth. "How did it go?" he asks, sinking back into his chair.

Spider sucks on the soggy Belomorkanal glued to his lower lip. "The fire door was open like he said, *pakhan*. There was no cops in sight. No dog barking neither. The sixers and me, we rigged the Studebaker that does not need a new carburetor, for good measure we rigged another of his cars, then as the hour was almost expired we got our asses up the steel stairs to our pickup in the alleyway."

Timur, preoccupied, turns to Lice. "I haven't seen Roman in two days. Where is he?"

Lice shifts his considerable weight from one foot to the other. "Don't know, *pakhan*."

"What do you mean, you don't know? With Mika Rasputin dead and buried, I instructed you to keep an eye on my son."

"I kept an eye on him when he was here in Moscow, here in this building," Lice explains. "Roman is not a baby who needs his diaper changed, *pakhan*."

"Are you telling me he's not in Moscow?"

Lice blots beads of perspiration from his forehead with the back of his sleeve. "I am telling you his bed has not been slept in. I am telling you he is probably shacking up with a girl somewhere. He does not check in with me when he wants to get laid, *pakhan*."

"If he's with that Jew girl . . ." Timur takes several deep breaths to calm the bad temper rising in him like a riptide. Shaking his head in frustration, he turns his attention back to Spider. "When you say you *rigged* the vehicles, what precisely does that mean?"

Spider, relieved to be on the mine-free terrain of his expertise, crushes the cigarette under the heel of his shoe, then, noticing Timur's cold stare, quickly stoops and picks up the butt. He looks around for someplace to stash it; seeing none, he slips it into his jacket pocket. "I do not hold with fixing the plastic so it explodes when someone starts the motor, *pakhan*," he begins. "The sergeant major in my Black Sea Marine Brigade, he was a lapsed Muslim with the almond eyes of an Uzbek who trained me to blow up unlapsed Muslims in Afghanistan. Me, I was taught doing it that way would tip off the prosecutors to where the bomb was planted, which in this particular situation would lead to the two night watchmen with the Doberman, the night watchmen being ex–Sixth Bureau coppers would lead to this Axelrod character, and Axelrod would lead straight to me and Lice here. Which is how come I rigged the fireworks not to start until the engine heats up from driving. That way it blows up in the street."

"How long before the explosion?" Timur wants to know.

"Depending on the vehicle's speed, depending on what gear the car is in, in the seven vehicles I done already it took something between twenty minutes and half an hour." Spider grunts in self-satisfaction. "Which means the coppers will have a tough time figuring out if it was a bomb planted in a sewer or an anti-tank rocket fired from a roof or an accident with Semtex stashed in the Studebaker's steel ammunition boxes under the seats."

"Okay. I am well pleased with your work, Spider." Timur, his lips pursed thoughtfully, turns to Lice. "We've been together a long time."

"We have, *pakhan*."

"I need to know where Roman is."

"I will ask around."

"You do that."

Naum Caplan's brother Mordechai turns up at the breakfast table the next morning holding an ice pack to his jawbone. "Got a god-awful toothache," he tells his brother. "Been up all night eating aspirins."

"Call our dentist."

"What do you think I did when I got up this morning, for shit's sake?" Mordechai remarks testily. "Fucking secretary said they were booked solid through Tuesday next week. I took an appointment first thing Tuesday morning but I am not sure I can survive until then."

"Listen, I was going in for my annual checkup later this morning," Naum says. "Here's what we'll do: You take my rendezvous and I'll take your Tuesday rendezvous."

"You sure?"

"Sure I'm sure," Naum says. "My kid brother has a toothache. I don't."

"God, thanks, Naum." Mordechai scrapes back his chair. "You're saving my life."

"Where you off to? Drink your coffee at least."

"I need to find more aspirins."

"When you go to the dentist, take the Studebaker," the *pakhan* calls after Mordechai. "With Timur's Ossetes on the warpath, you cannot be too cautious these days."

18
TIMUR THE LAME: OSSETE SONS NEED TO STAND WITH THEIR FATHERS IN TIME OF WAR . . .

MOSCOW

Saturday, January 18, 1992

Lice sets up the small East German portable television and its antenna on Timur's desk and plugs it into a wall socket. "You will want to see this, *pakhan*," he says. "They ran it on the twelve o'clock news, so they are probably going to show it again on the one o'clock."

"I do not watch television," Timur reminds his enforcer.

"You will make an exception for this," Lice predicts.

Timur the Lame focuses on the flickering screen as the camera slowly pans past the debris of a Great Patriotic War armored personnel carrier scattered over Komsomolskaya Square across from the Leningradsky railroad terminal. The camera zooms in on a puddle of blood and a galosh with the stump of a foot still in it. Tarpaulins have been thrown over the three corpses in the gutter. A fire hydrant damaged by the explosion gushes water along one curb. A reddish scarf of smoke hangs over the two dozen or so bystanders watching grimly from behind the police crime scene barrier. "Luckily nobody in the street was close when the car blew up," a reporter whispers excitedly into his microphone. "The death toll could have been tragically higher."

The news program cuts back to the studio. "The three victims, all males, were said to be soldiers in Naum Caplan's *vory v zakone* organization," the female anchor, peering into the camera with heavily made-up eyes, recounts. "One of them has been identified as Caplan's younger brother, Mordechai. Police have confirmed that Caplan himself was not in the vehicle, an American Studebaker personnel carrier vintage 1943. Questions abound. Was the explosion an unfortunate accident or a settling of scores between competing gangs vying for a bigger piece of the post-Soviet pie? The chief of the Sixth Bureau of the Organized Crime Control Department, O. Axelrod, leans toward accident. He suggests that unstable RDX stowed in the armored car might have exploded when the Studebaker hit a pothole on Komsomolskaya Square. A top official at the state prosecutor's office, speaking off the record as he was not authorized to talk about the incident, said his people were convinced that the blast has all the earmarks of a meticulously planned homicide. If they are correct, chances are there will be more American-style gangland murders in Moscow before the Great Turf War is over. In other news today—"

Lice reaches across the table and snaps off the television. The screen fills with electronic snow, which gradually fades to pitch black. "A good day's work, huh, *pakhan*?" Lice says hopefully.

Timur, a pulse beating visibly in his thin neck, barely controls the cold rage poisoning him. "Escapes me how you can think this was a good day's work," he declares in an icy undertone. "It will not have been lost on you that Caplan was not in the Studebaker."

"He was supposed to be going to the dentist," Lice explains, a trace of a whine in his voice. "We paid the receptionist to tip us off next time Caplan had a rendezvous. Next time was this time. Caplan definitely had a date with the dentist. Being that we know for a fact the Studebaker was the only vehicle he ever rode in, the hit looked to be in the bag." Lice produces a nervous giggle. "Not my fault if it turned out the wrong Caplan was on his way to the tooth fairy."

Timur makes his way to the window and stares out at Moscow through panes streaked with the morning's drizzle. "We are back where we started," he murmurs. "Caplan is not going to swallow his pride, not to mention his bile. Count on it—he is going to want revenge for the death of his brother."

"Only tell me what you want me to do, *pakhan*, and I will die trying."

"I was under the impression that I told you already: I want you—I *need you*—to find Roman. Ossete sons need to stand with their fathers in time of war." Lice starts to backpedal toward the door. Timur calls after him, "Take the damn television with you when you go."

The English delivery van, painted coal black with *Sweet Tooth Ltd* scrawled in beautiful gold calligraphic letters on each of its sides, pulls up parallel to the gate of Timur's Lenin Hills mansion. Lowering the driver's window, a young man dressed in the Russians' idea of English livery leans out and hits the intercom button. "It's me, Timofey, with your boss's weekly chocolate ration," he shouts into the speaker box.

"Beats me how the fuck can you drive with the wheel on the wrong side," the brigadier on security duty says over the intercom.

Timofey laughs. "It's actually not all that different once you get the hang of it."

With a grating squeal, the heavy gate starts to slowly swing open. "I'm sending one of the sixers down to get it," the tinny voice on the intercom announces.

Timofey fetches the box, gift wrapped in fancy black fabric with the Sweet Tooth logo embossed on the blood-red ribbon, and hands it to the young Ossete who turns up at the gate.

The sixer, a green recruit who is the second cousin of one of Timur's veteran Ossete enforcers, carries the box down to the basement security room. The brigadier on duty, keeping an eye on the bank of small security screens, is listening to a news program in English on Radio Maximum. "Didn't know you spoke American," the sixer remarks.

"Don't," the brigadier says.

"So how come you're listening to Maximum in American?"

"News is easier to ignore when you don't understand it," the brigadier explains seriously.

"Makes sense," the sixer agrees. He sets the box down on the x-ray belt. "Hope to hell the radiation don't melt the *pakhan*'s chocolates," he says, passing the box through the x-ray machine. He and the brigadier study the image frozen on the screen. "Can this contraption really look right through things?" he asks.

"See for yourself, kid."

"So what does a bomb look like, then?"

"If it's a plastic bomb, they can shape it to look like anything—a book or a tangerine or a liverwurst sandwich."

"Where in Moscow would you find liverwurst to make a sandwich?"

"It would not be real liverwurst, kid. It would be plastic liverwurst."

"So how can you tell if it's a bomb sandwich or a real sandwich?"

"If it's a bomb sandwich, it needs to have a fuse to explode."

"Ah. A long wick that's sizzling away to beat the band, like when you set off a firecracker."

"More like a clock that is fixed to go off in a certain amount of time than a firecracker wick, kid. A clock, anything that looks like a clock, is suspicious."

The sixer retrieves the box of Sweet Tooth Ltd. chocolates from the x-ray belt. "This sure is a lot of chocolate for one person," he says.

"Our enforcer Lice, who did time with the old man in Labor Colony Number Forty, went and told me all Timur's Ossetes got cigarette rations but the *pakhan*, even in the godforsaken Kungur, managed to cadge a weekly supply of chocolates."

The young sixer whistles through his teeth. "Musta cost him an arm and a leg."

"Not sure he paid for it back then," the brigadier allows, snickering. "Not sure he pays for it now neither. Us Ossetes are the ones who supply the roof to this limey Sweet Tooth outfit." The brigadier slips back into his swivel chair facing the bank of screens. "You need to get your ass upstairs, kid, and deliver the chocolates to the *pakhan*. It may put him in a good mood for five or ten minutes."

19
TIMUR THE LAME: THE GREEK PREDICTED SWEET TOOTH WOULD *K-K-KILL* ME . . .

MOSCOW

Sunday, January 19, 1992

The sixteen-year-old cleaning girl Zhukaeva, the illegitimate daughter of Lice's cousin Khetag from Tskhinvali, discovers Timur the Lame unconscious in his narrow army-surplus metal bed, his eyes shut, his mouth gaping open, a half-eaten chocolate clasped in his reedy fingers, dry vomit staining the pillow under his head. Leaning closer, the girl can make out gold glistening in one of the *pakhan*'s teeth. Zhukaeva, clutching the week's supply of Timur's vitamins and the morning mail to her apron, stands frozen at the foot of the bed desperately trying to figure out what not to do. Remembering how such things were done back in Tskhinvali, she decides she needs to not touch the corpse lest she catch what he died of. She decides she needs to not scream for help lest she awaken the brigadiers sleeping in the attic bunk room under the mansion's roof. She creeps out of the room on tiptoes so as not to disturb the eternal sleep of the dead *pakhan*. Noiselessly closing the bedroom door behind her, she grips the banister on the staircase and begins to whisper, "Help, oh help, the *pakhan* is murdered."

Lice, who by chance is passing on the landing beneath her, hears whispering and, climbing the flight two steps at a time, says to her, "For God's sake, girl, what's not right?"

Zhukaeva looks at him with wide, frightened eyes, then parts her lips to report the murder. Unable to locate her vocal cords, she panics and stabs an index finger at the *pakhan*'s door.

"Speak up, girl!"

"The *pakhan* is murdered," she finally manages to whisper.

"How murdered? *Where murdered!*"

"In his bed," the girl says out loud.

Lice lunges for the door and, catching sight of the half-eaten chocolate and the vomit-stained pillow, flings his hulking body across the room to the army bed. Zhukaeva, at the door, begins to sob softly. "Please, God, have mercy on the *pakhan*'s soul as it makes its way through the valley of the shadow of death," she murmurs.

Lice rushes into the small bathroom off the bedroom and comes back with the Mercedes side-view mirror Timur uses for shaving. He holds it to the *pakhan*'s bloodless lips, then, spying a trace of vapor on the mirror, cries out, "He is still alive!" And he runs to the stairwell to do what the village girl new to the big city dared not do: wake the brigadiers, wake the enforcers and the sixers, wake the neighborhood, wake the dead and the living in Moscow. "For the love of God," he shrieks into the stairwell, "somebody call the emergency service! Our *pakhan* has been poisoned."

On the seventh floor of Moscow City Clinical Hospital No. 63, Lice and Spare Rib take turns guarding the door, one of them inside the room, the other outside. Timur, snoring fitfully, lies on a raised hospital bed with wires and drains fastened to his naked body by strips of adhesive. The pale glimmer of a rising three-quarter moon is visible through the rain-stained window. A visibly exhausted female doctor, wearing a white surgical smock stained with dried blood, studies the screen monitoring Timur's vital signs.

"Tell me he is going to pull through," Lice demands.

The doctor swallows a yawn. Lice, furious, blurts out, "Excuse me if I am boring you with my fucking questions."

"You need to calm down, Mr. Whatever Your Name Is."

"My friends call me Lice. My enemies too."

"Is Lice your Christian name?"

"It's my pagan name."

The doctor rolls her eyes. "Right. Here's the thing, Mr. Lice, I've been on my feet since six this morning. To answer your question, maybe he'll pull through, maybe he won't. It all depends."

"On what does it depend?"

"On the general state of his health to begin with. On his body's ability to fight off acute liver disease, which is a classic complication in cases of poisoning. We're waiting for the lab to analyze the chocolate sample and identify the poison. That can take forty-eight hours." She checks the metal logbook attached to the foot of the bed. "The ER doctor on duty when you brought him in this morning prescribed an antiepileptic drip to stop his seizures and that seems to have worked. The patient has also been getting atropine via an intravenous drip to neutralize potential pesticide poisoning. If his condition deteriorates, if he appears to be suffering physical pain, as a last resort we will put him in a medically induced coma." She glances sideways at Lice. "Are you his son?"

"More than a son," Lice murmurs.

"The ward nurse told me you and your friend outside are armed. Are you armed?"

"With hope."

The doctor flashes a tired smile. "Okay. Don't lose hope. The next twenty-four hours should tell one way or another. If he survives the night, if we can identify the poison and administer a specific antidote . . ." She lets the sentence trail off.

Sinking back into the bedside chair, Lice notices Timur's lips trembling. He appears to be trying to form words. Lice scrapes the chair closer to the bed and leans over him, his ear almost touching the *pakhan*'s lips. "What are you trying to say?"

"Gdye—"

"Where? Where what?"

"*Gdye* . . . Ro . . . Ro . . .?"

"Roman? Is that what you're trying to say?"

Timur blinks in confusion.

"I wish I knew where Roman is, *pakhan*."

"Gdye . . . ya?"

"You are in the hospital, *pakhan*."

"Why hospital? I . . . sick?"

Lice timidly takes hold of the *pakhan*'s clammy hand. "You were poisoned, *pakhan*. It was the chocolates."

"Poison . . ." Timur the Lame coughs up a shred of a laugh. "The Greek . . ."

"What about the Greek?"

"Back . . . Labor Col-ny Forty . . . he pre . . . pre . . . *dicted* damn sweet tooth"—a whistle escapes from Timur's bad nostril—"would *k-k-kill* me."

20

ROMAN: AFTER I BURY MY FATHER I WILL BURY THE PERSON WHO MURDERED HIM . . .

LIVADIYA PALACE, YALTA

Monday, January 20, 1992

A ghostly morning haze is just beginning to burn off as Roman and Yulia set off along the Tsar's Path to explore the cliff that snakes between the bedraggled lawns and hedges of Livadiya and the town of Yalta, some three or so kilometers to the north. Trekking along the dirt path, they can hear the waves far below breaking against the rocky shore at the foot of the cliff, long before the haze dissipates and they catch sight of the sea. Roman walks several steps ahead but when the sun breaks through, Yulia, pointing excitedly at the great dome of the Alexander Nevsky Cathedral towering over Yalta in the distance, catches up with him. "I was there once when I was nine or ten," she exclaims. "It was the first time I managed to sweet-talk my father into letting me go with a Pioneer group from school. Oh God, I remember the cathedral, I remember the sea splashing our feet when we ran across the seawall, I remember our hostel was on a street named Roosevelt. The name didn't sound Russian and I had no idea who he was. Our Pioneer scoutmaster told us this Roosevelt was a dreadful imperialist who loathed our beloved *Dyadya* Stalin."

"You didn't swallow that *beloved Uncle Stalin* claptrap, I hope."

"I was nine years old, for Christ's sake."

"When I was nine years old, like my father, like his Ossetes, I despised your beloved Uncle Stalin."

"He's not *my* Uncle Stalin, Roman." She catches the laughter in his eyes. "You're making fun of me but I'll survive. I did have a life-changing epiphany in Yalta and it wasn't discovering that Stalin was my uncle. After the monitors shut us in the hostel's attic dormitory for the night, one of the older Pioneers, she must have been all of fourteen, produced a lipstick and, in the pitch-darkness illuminated by the feeble beams of our flashlights, she painted the lips of all of us younger girls bright red. It was my introduction to lipstick."

Following the path, Roman and Yulia skirt a peat marsh and what's left of an ancient peat works, its roof timbers and tiles caving into the derelict building. "So did you like your lips painted the same color as a fire engine?" Roman asks.

"Like it? I loved it, Roman! Lipstick, my God! I think I got my first inkling that there might be life after childhood. When I caught sight of my reflection in a window, I suddenly saw what I might look like when I grew up." She hooks an arm through his. "Do *you* like my lips painted like a fire engine?"

Roman stops in his tracks. "The first time I met you, it was at your midnight birthday party in the Metropole, your lips were painted the same color as your short ice-skating skirt. I am very attracted to your lips, whether they are bright red or not," he says very seriously. "I thought I might have convinced you of this." He spots the taunting smile in her eyes. "Now you're making fun of me."

Farther along the Tsar's Path, the trail winds through a dense stand of white birches, their stooped trunks leaning away from the prevailing sea winds. Roman persists: "Tell me something—why *do* girls wear lipstick?"

His questions are starting to irritate Yulia. "Why are you all of a sudden obsessed with lipstick?" she demands. "Girls wear lipstick to attract attention, of course."

"And why do some girls *not* wear lipstick?"

"To attract attention," Yulia replies with an edgy laugh. "If a girl wears lipstick, you notice. If she doesn't, you notice. I honestly don't know where this conversation is going. Your questions sound right out of a medieval inquisition when they burned women at the stake for the crime of being women. Like most males of the species, you really don't comprehend the female of the species."

"I am trying to comprehend the female of the species. If I have it right, what you're saying is it all boils down to a need, to a craving, to be noticed?"

"Jesus, Roman, are men so different? Why do some of you wear a gold chain around your neck or a ring on your pinkie? Why do you wear an RAF bomber jacket, which may be the only one of its kind in all of Russia? You want to be noticed! Why do you wear a fancy Swiss wristwatch that tells the phases of the moon? If you're really curious about the phases of the moon, look at the moon, for Christ's sake."

"I didn't mean to start an argument."

"My luck, I've fallen for a lip fetishist! Hey, you're so fixated on my lips, you obviously haven't been paying attention to the rest of me. You didn't notice I cleaned the lint out of my belly button."

Roman tries to defuse the tension with a quip. "Not much you can do about your breasts pointing in different directions."

"I can go in different directions, which is what I seem to be doing since I met you." She turns on her heel. "Let's head back. We should have had breakfast before we set out."

"I thought the gusts from the sea would give you an appetite."

"Arguing with you about lipstick has given me an appetite."

Yulia's uncle Olezka and Anthony are sitting across from each other at one end of the long refectory table that monks in a Crimean monastery once used to make bread. Ruts scar the thick oak where they pounded the sourdough for centuries. As neither Olezka nor Anthony speaks a language the other understands, both of them are relieved to see the two Tsar's Path hikers turn up. Anthony points with his chin to the television in a corner that Olezka switched on when he came into the breakfast room off the palace's great kitchen. "Can you get him to turn the damn thing off?" Anthony asks Roman.

Olezka seems to have gotten the gist of what Anthony said. "Kindly inform him," he says to Roman in very elegant Russian, "that we are in my house, not his. Kindly inform him that I am in the habit of watching the morning news to see if war has broken out somewhere in the world the night before."

Olezka's cleaning woman, an acne-scarred peasant from a village in the hills behind Yalta, appears at the kitchen door struggling with a tray loaded with food. Roman leaps up to help and, relieving her of the tray, sets it on the table. The cleaning woman fills the breakfast plates with blinis and sour cream, pork sausages and slices of raw red onion, which Yulia passes around. Olezka pours a sweet Crimean white wine known for its whiskey kick into thick kitchen tumblers. "Wine for breakfast!" Anthony exults. "Please tell my host, his television addiction notwithstanding, I am toying with the idea of moving to Livadiya permanently."

"You will need to become fluent in Russian if you want to live here," Roman says.

"Hadn't thought of that angle. Scratch my moving here permanently."

Roman is halfway through his blini when something on the morning news catches his ear. He hurries over to the television to turn up the volume and crouches in front of the set. Yulia stops eating and swivels in her seat.

"Mob violence in Moscow has claimed yet another victim, Timur Monsurov, a legendary figure in *vory v zakone* circles known as Timur the Lame, after the fourteenth-century Mongol warrior Tamerlane who founded the Timurid Empire on the Eurasian Steppe. Monsurov, believed to be in his early seventies, reportedly served twenty-two years in various Soviet detention camps and was said to be the *pakhan* of the Moscow-based Ossete *vory*. Moscow municipal police are awaiting the forensic report but expect it to confirm that Monsurov was poisoned in his fortress-home in the Lenin Hills just days after the booby-trapped murder, in Komsomolskaya Square, of Mordechai Caplan, his arch-enemy's brother. A senior official in the Sixth Bureau of the Organized Crime Control Department, which monitors crime families operating in Russia's urban areas, predicted that Timur Monsurov's assassination would unleash a tsunami of violence as the various *vory v zakone* clashing for control of territory settle scores. 'The positive thing about a mob war is it gives business to our undertakers,' declared the official, who was not authorized to speak about the murder of Timur Monsurov publicly. In Vladivostok, meanwhile . . ."

Yulia, crouching beside Roman, places a cool palm on the nape of his neck. "I am so sorry," she whispers.

Swatting away her arm, he pushes himself to his feet. "Not

half as sorry as I, his son, his seed. If only I had been there . . . *If only* seems to be the story of my life."

She stands too. "What are you going to do?"

"Anthony," Roman calls across the room, "can you fly me back to Moscow?"

"I suppose I could, old boy."

Yulia tries to put her arms around Roman's neck but he pushes her roughly away. "That's it!" she cries, startled. "What about *us*?"

Roman grasps her roughly by the shoulders. "There is no us," he informs her in an undertone. "There is a you and there is a me. And the me is going back to bury his father."

"And after you bury your father? What then?"

"After I bury my father I will bury the person who murdered him."

Yulia backs away from him, her eyes wide with foreboding. "There are parts of *you* I haven't explored yet," she murmurs. "You didn't fall all that far from the tree after all, Roman Timurovich. You are, like your late father, Ossete to the marrow of your bones."

"There was a time when I thought I could escape my destiny, Yulia. I didn't run fast enough. I have become the man I was afraid of becoming. Like it or not, I am the son of Timur the Lame." A line that Mel Gibson's Prince Hamlet spoke on the movie screen in London finds an echo in Roman's brain and, looking away, he utters it: "From this time forth, my thoughts be bloody."

Roman uses the telephone in Olezka's cramped cubbyhole of an office just off the palace entrance to call the basement security room in Timur's mansion. "This is Roman," he growls into the receiver. "I need to speak to Lice or Spare Rib."

"I'll put you through, Roman. About your father—"

"Put me through, damn it."

After an eternity of minutes Spare Rib comes on the line. "Roman, Roman, I am miserable about Timur—"

"You need to be miserable, Spare Rib—miserable you didn't protect him. It was Caplan's crowd, wasn't it?" He doesn't wait for an answer. "How in hell did he manage to poison my father under his own roof?"

"The Sweet Tooth people delivered chocolates, like they do every week. Caplan somehow got to the *pakhan*'s chocolates. We scanned them like we always do but the x-rays don't pick up on poison."

"Did he suffer?"

"When he looked as if he was in pain, the hospital people went and put him into a coma." Spare Rib catches his breath. "He never woke up, Roman."

There is a long silence on the line. Each can hear the other breathing. Spare Rib finally says, "The cops got their forensics back this morning. They told Lice and me we could claim the *pakhan*'s body. What should we do with it—with him?"

"I remember him saying something about wanting to be cremated, not buried. Organize it. I am coming back, I'll be in Moscow tonight. We will scatter his ashes, Spare Rib. Then we will figure out how to give the crematorium more work."

21

ROMAN: A LOT WILL BE RIDING ON HOW WELL WE COORDINATE THE RAID . . .

MOSCOW

Later Monday

Glancing occasionally out the cockpit window to be sure they are not flying into the side of a mountain, Anthony spends most of the six-hour flight back to Moscow fiddling with dials as he pores over the instruction manual for his newfangled radio beacon navigation system. "Eureka!" he exclaims three and a quarter hours into the flight, fine-tuning one of the dials. "I think I raised Archangelsk."

"We're not going to Archangelsk," Roman remarks dryly.

Anthony, cheerful as always, says, "You're not thinking out of the box, old boy. Archangelsk is in the right direction. Follow Archangelsk and Bob's your uncle."

Flying just above a thick carpet of stratocumulus cotton into Moscow's airspace, Anthony finally manages to tune in the airfield that they started off from four days before. "Bloody hell, I think I locked onto Bolshoye Gryzlovo!" he cries excitedly. He checks the petrol gauges on the Cessna's instrument panel.

"None too soon," he mutters, talking more to himself than to his two passengers, who haven't exchanged a word since they took off from Simferopol Vokzal—Roman catnapping in the copilot's seat, Yulia wide awake and staring sightlessly out the window behind the pilot. "Bloody main tank is twinkling on empty; with a bit of luck, there's enough left in the starboard wing tank to bring us home," Anthony informs himself.

"Sorry. What did you say?"

"Nothing." Gripping the yoke with both hands, Anthony drops the Cessna's nose and knifes into and through the stratocumulus carpet before emerging three kilometers from the airstrip. Shutting one eye and squinting through the other, he lines the plane up with Bolshoye Gryzlovo's single runway. The tips of Stalin Gothic towers, some thirty kilometers distant, stab through Moscow's veil of pollution. Ricocheting off the tarmac several times, the Cessna finally settles onto the runway and taxis over to the dilapidated building that serves as a terminal.

Lice and Spare Rib, alerted to Roman's arrival by the airport's control tower, are on hand to meet the plane. "I s'pose this is goodbye," Anthony says as Spare Rib throws Roman's duffel into the trunk of the Range Rover. Anthony leans toward Yulia and plants a timid kiss on each of her pale cheeks. "No tears, please," he quips.

"What did he say?" she demands. When Roman translates, she declares with a bitter edge to her voice, "Kindly inform him I only cry over spilt milk."

"What did she say?" Anthony insists.

"She said she hopes you'll have good weather on your flight back to England," Roman tells him. He pulls Anthony aside. "Thank you, Anthony—best thing that ever happened to me was winding up in your flat in London."

Anthony, embarrassed by displays of emotion, clears his

throat. "Can't be a cakewalk coming home to bury a father, old boy. Hope your Russians treat you better than we Brits did."

Lice comes over and puts a hand on Roman's shoulder. "We need to hit the road."

Roman turns to Yulia. "Can I at least give you a lift into town?"

"Thanks but no thanks. There was a time when I wanted everything from you. Now I want nothing, not even a ride into the city."

"Listen, I'm sorry I disappointed you."

"Fuck you, Roman from another planet."

"I am definitely fucked," he agrees wholeheartedly.

Neither of them is able to produce a smile.

Ignoring stop signs, running red lights on the avenue, the Range Rover races east on Volgogradskiy Prospekt. Lice drives, Spare Rib rides shotgun, Roman sits in the back with the earthen urn on his lap, one hand on the rim to keep it from spilling as the car swerves around slower-moving trucks, the fingers of his other hand massaging his eyes to ward off the sudden exhaustion that is as much mental as physical. "Fuck you," he mutters to himself. "Fuck me."

Spare Rib twists in his seat. "What you say, *pakhan*?"

"Why do you address me as *pakhan*?"

"With Timur dead and cremated, it's you the capo of the Ossetes' *vory*, Roman. You are the only one who can fill his shoes. We need you to bring the war home to the enemy who went and murdered our *vozhd*."

Roman tightens his grip on the urn. "First I will scatter my father's ashes. Then we will devise a scheme to provide the crematorium with more bodies—something that will give satisfaction to the chief of the Sixth Bureau of the Organized Crime Control Department, O. Axelrod."

The Range Rover speeds past a signpost marking the outskirts of the town of Dzerzhinskiy, and a smaller sign under it giving directions to the Russian Orthodox monastery of Saint Nicholas the Miracle Worker. Lice glances at Roman in the rearview mirror. "Out of curiosity, why Dzerzhinskiy?" he asks.

"Timur took me here once when I was a boy. He told me I could see Siberia from the top of the monastery's bell tower."

"And did you? See Siberia even though it's two thousand kilometers from here?"

"Yes, definitely. I saw the great frozen steppe, I saw white polar bears struggling through knee-deep snow, I saw a mother fox snuggling with her babies to keep them warm in a nest of leaves and twigs."

Lice starts to laugh, then clamps his mouth shut when Spare Rib elbows him in the ribs.

After a while Spare Rib turns in his seat again. "How old were you when you saw Siberia from the bell tower, *pakhan*?"

"I don't remember how old I was—ten maybe, maybe eleven. I only remember Siberia."

Arctic gusts graze the monastery as Lice pulls up in the lee of its four domes. Roman zips the RAF bomber jacket up to his neck and, with Spare Rib in tow, heads for the white bell tower with the gold dome crowning it. A bearded Orthodox monk wearing a thick black *kamilavka*, the sleeves of woolen long johns protruding on his wrists, guards the ground-floor alcove giving onto the steel staircase. Annoyed that neither man reaches down to touch his knuckles to the ground at his feet, he eyes the earthen urn in Roman's arms. "Bell tower's not open to the public," he informs them.

Spare Rib places a palm on the monk's kamilavka, coaxing him back a few steps. "It is now, holy brother," he informs him.

Roman starts up the winding staircase, the urn clasped to

his chest. Winded, he reaches the top and leans for a moment on the guardrail to catch his breath. Curiously, the wooden milk crate on which he once climbed, the better to see Siberia, is still there. Roman peers out, hoping to catch a glimpse of the Siberia he invented as a boy, but all he can make out is the blinding darkness of the starless night seeping through the dense shadows of the forest. He checks the phase of the moon on his Patek Philippe; the full moon that should have been visible above the horizon at sunset is missing from the night sky, concealed behind the murky stratocumulus soup the Cessna flew through as it approached Bolshoye Gryzlovo.

Filling his lungs with the stingingly cold air howling past his ears, Roman rests the urn on the guardrail for a long moment, as if he is loath to part with his father—loath to part *from* his father. "What the hell," he mutters as he lifts the urn and spills the ashes into the starless night. Blotting with the back of his wrist tears that freeze on his face before they can fall to the ground, he sets the urn on the milk crate and, gripping the steel banister with one hand, starts back down the bell tower.

The new *pakhan* presides over the council of war in Timur the Lame's second-floor dining room. The large framed photograph of Roman's fifth birthday party is conspicuous on the wall behind him. An architect's plan of the Narodnaya Hotel is spread open on the oval table, weighted down on its four corners with salt and pepper and dry-dill shakers and a bowl filled with sugar swiped from restaurants. Lice, Spare Rib, Spider, three brigadiers, five enforcers, and a young sixer who has just been promoted to enforcer crowd around the table.

"So where did you wind up scattering your lamented father's ashes?" the Greek, monitoring the war council from his usual perch on the windowsill, inquires.

"In Siberia," Roman informs him.

The Greek appears confused. "How in Siberia?"

"You heard the man," Spare Rib growls. "He said in Siberia. End of conversation."

Lice kicks off the council of war, setting out the intelligence they have collected on the Narodnaya Hotel. "Naum Caplan rents the top two floors," he begins. "We have a cleaning girl from Timur's village of Areshperani on the inside. She can pass for Russian—she is divorced from a Russian husband but still uses his name. Thanks to her we've been saving string on Caplan's operation for months. According to our girl, Caplan lodges thirty-eight of his soldiers, roughly half of them with wives or girlfriends, on the fifteenth floor. Eighteen of his senior brigadiers, as well as two armorers, both Byelorussian Jews from the legendary Fifth Spetsnaz Brigade, and an accountant who shares a room with a male companion, along with Caplan himself, live on the sixteenth, or top, floor. It is this floor that will be the target of our raid." Lice points with a chopstick to the sixteenth floor on the plan. "Caplan has a suite consisting of four rooms here at the end of the hallway. His daughter, name of Yulia, has a three-room suite across the hall from her condemned father."

"Does Caplan have a wife?" one of the enforcers asks.

"He has a common-law wife, his third, an Israelite woman eighteen years younger than his second, but she is in Vilnius right now caring for a sick father."

"Assuming we can infiltrate the hotel without attracting attention, how do we get our asses up to the top floor?" a brigadier wants to know. "Staircase?"

"The main hotel staircase is fitted with security cameras on every floor, the screens are monitored by hotel security people in a room behind the check-in desk, the images from the cameras are piped up to the fifteenth floor and monitored in one of the rooms by Caplan's people. Getting twelve Ossetes up the main staircase without sirens going off is a nonstarter."

"What about the elevators?"

Lice points out the ground-floor elevator alcove. "There's a bank of four elevators here just off the lobby but only one of them is programmed to stop on the fifteenth or sixteenth floor."

Roman looks at Lice. "You've skipped a juicy detail."

"What detail would that be, *pakhan*?"

The two exchange knowing half-smiles. This is the first time Lice, who was with the first Ossete *pakhan*, Timur the Lame, in Strict Regime Corrective Labor Colony No. 40, has addressed Roman as *pakhan*. "The elevator, my friend," Roman reminds him. "Tell the boys what they do with it at night."

"The elevator, right." Lice turns back to the Ossetes around the table. "Our cleaning girl reported for work twenty minutes early one morning and tried to summon the elevator so she could get a jump on emptying the hall ashtrays on Caplan's floor—Caplan seems to have complained about the smell of cigarette ends. No matter how many times she pressed the button, she could see from the light above the door that it was stuck on the sixteenth. When she reported the problem to the desk, the night manager told her the Jews wedged the elevator door open with a chair at night to make sure it remained locked on their floor."

"You still have not answered my question," the Ossete brigadier insists. "If the staircase is off the table and Caplan has disabled the single elevator programmed to reach his floor, how do *we* get up there?"

"We will go up to the sixteenth on the fire staircase," Lice announces. He points it out on the plan. "There are no security cameras, but there is one potential complication: The fire doors are chained shut on the inside on both of Caplan's floors. We figure that is not going to slow us down."

"The fire door on the sixteenth is where Spider gets to earn his keep," Roman says. He doesn't bother to finish the thought. Everyone understands that Spider, with the tattoo of a sputtering fuse under his right eye, is the Ossetes' bomb maker.

One of the enforcers raises a hand. "We are not in kindergarten here," Roman tells him. "Speak up."

"Even supposing we manage to get up to the sixteenth floor, Caplan's brigadiers, who outnumber us, are going to come out shooting once the attack begins. We will be outgunned—"

Lice interrupts him. "They can shoot all they want but they can't hit what they don't see," he says. "We had a stroke of luck," he explains. "Our Ossete girl was vacuuming rooms on the sixteenth floor during an electrical storm. When the fuse blew, cutting off the electricity, she rode the elevator, which worked on a separate circuit, down to the basement with the hotel's handyman. Thanks to her, we know the master fuse box is in a small locked room next to the baggage storage cage in the basement. A sign on the door reads *Hotel Personnel Only.* The metal box is padlocked but a crowbar will take care of that. In the fuse box, each floor of the hotel is marked. The master interrupter for Caplan's floor is the bottom one in the fuse box and labeled with the number sixteen in red."

Roman gestures to the young sixer. "It will be your job to break into this locked basement room, Pavel. You will need to synchronize your wristwatch, to the second, with Spider and trip the fuse on the sixteenth floor at the stroke of five. Not a second before, not a second after."

The sixer, who has written home boasting about being promoted to enforcer, nods vigorously. "Count on me, *pakhan.*"

"We will all be counting on you," Roman tells him. "A lot will be riding on how well we coordinate the raid."

"*Pakhan*, Caplan is bound to have eyes and ears in the

lobby," one of the senior Ossete brigadiers remarks. "How the hell can we get thirteen of us, and our artillery, into the hotel without tripping alarms?"

All eyes are on the new *pakhan*. "Here's how," he says. And leaning over the architect's plan, he explains his scheme.

22
ROMAN AND YULIA: THE DÉNOUEMENT, FROM THE FRENCH *UNKNOT* . . .

THE NARODNAYA HOTEL, MOSCOW

Tuesday, January 21, 1992

The late-afternoon guests milling in the Narodnaya's lobby take little notice of the arrival of musicians carrying violin and viola and cello cases. They all wear ankle-length overcoats with scarves wrapped around their necks and skintight gloves that, curiously, they don't take off indoors. Roman, dressed in a tie and suit jacket under his father's cashmere overcoat, makes his way to the front desk and punches the bell to get the attention of the female clerk slipping cards with the hotel's dinner menu into mailboxes. "Evening," she says, turning. "What can I do for you?"

"My name is Lipschitz. I'm the impresario of the Vladivostok Chamber Orchestra." He flashes an internal Soviet identity card but the clerk barely looks at it. "We are booked into the Tchaikovsky tomorrow evening," Roman says. "I phoned yesterday to reserve six double rooms and one single, also your auditorium for a rehearsal tomorrow morning."

The clerk, with a name tag identifying her as Zinaïda pinned over the breast pocket of her crimson jacket, ducks her head to check the screen on the shelf. "No problem, we have rooms reserved for you on the third floor, all of them equipped with a TV and a minibar." She looks past Roman at the musicians carrying the instruments. "Are your bags still on the bus?"

"The airline lost them somewhere between Vladivostok and Moscow," Roman explains with an irritated grimace. "They promised to deliver them to us tonight, tomorrow morning at the latest. They better find our gear—I don't see my people performing in street clothes."

"Will you and your colleagues be dining with us tonight?"

"They fed us on the flight from Vladivostok and we have a big day ahead of us tomorrow," Roman tells her. "I think we prefer to get a good night's sleep."

"Understood." Zinaïda clears her throat. "May I ask how you will be paying for your stay at the Narodnaya?"

"Do you have a prejudice against cash?"

The clerk is unable to suppress a laugh. "We certainly don't, Mr. Lipschitz. Will that be US dollars or rubles?"

"US dollars."

Zinaïda bends to look at the screen. "Seven rooms at thirty dollars a night comes to four hundred twenty for two nights."

"On the phone I was quoted a group rate," Roman says.

She checks the screen again. "The four hundred twenty is the group rate, Mr. Lipschitz. As you are not using a credit card, hotel policy requires payment on checking in. Room service and the minibar can be settled on checking out. The second-floor auditorium is offered gratis, compliments of the house. Would you mind if some guests or staff sit in on your rehearsal?"

"Not at all," Roman says. He opens his shoulder satchel on the counter and produces a thick manila envelope. With difficulty, for he is still wearing street gloves, he begins to count out crisp new twenty-dollar bills.

"That would be easier if you took off your gloves," Zinaïda suggests.

"My hands are cold," Roman tells her.

She glances over his shoulder at the orchestra's musicians. "They must have cold hands too," she notes.

"You have to understand, string players are obsessed with keeping their fingers warm," Roman explains as he pushes the pile of dollars across the counter. "Because you have nice teeth, this is for you," he says, adding a twenty to the pile.

Zinaïda smiles her thanks as she fills in a receipt, stamps it with the hotel seal, and passes it, along with seven room keys, to Roman. "Thank you for choosing the Narodnaya for the Vladivostok Chamber Orchestra's stay in Moscow. And good luck with your concert, Mr. Lipschitz. I do hope your bags get here in time for your performance tomorrow."

"Our performance tomorrow will not be the same if they don't," Roman says with a grim smile.

The oversize Samsonite, with a plastic label that identifies it as belonging to a Narodnaya guest named Lipschitz, is delivered to the hotel at eleven fifteen by two men in a black Range Rover with tinted windows. The young night porter wheeling it up to Lipschitz's room on the third floor grumbles, "What do you have in here, bricks?"

"It's filled with musical scores, that's why it's so heavy," Roman explains, tipping the porter, who holds the five-dollar bill up to the light.

"Who is the dude with the beard?" he asks.

"One of their presidents, name of Lincoln."

"What is Mr. Lincoln worth in Russian rubles?"

"Something like four hundred, maybe a bit more. It changes from day to day."

On his way out the young porter turns at the door and regards Mr. Lipschitz. "None of my business, but how come you're still wearing gloves?"

"My hands are cold. I have bad circulation."

The porter accepts this with a bob of his chin. "They got pills for that—my grandma takes them," he says. As Roman seems more interested in the Samsonite, the porter shrugs and closes the door behind him.

Roman uses the house phone to summon Spider, who turns up to help him unpack the hand grenades and spare thirty-round magazines and plastic explosive, along with the night-vision goggles in bubble wrap. Once everything is laid out on the bed, the Ossetes come by, one by one, to collect the weaponry. "Tell me you didn't forget to bring along a crowbar," Roman, fretting over details, remarks to the sixer who was recently promoted to enforcer.

"Not to worry, *pakhan*—it was stashed in my violin case alongside the Nagant with a tennis ball fitted onto the barrel," the boy says. "The *Hotel Personnel Only* door, the fuse box, the master fuse for floor number sixteen, the stroke of five—I been over it a hundred times in my head."

Roman, fully dressed, is catnapping on top of the bedspread when the alarm on his Patek Philippe buzzes softly. He glances at the dials. "Four thirty already," he mutters to himself. He pads into the bathroom and splashes cold water on his face. "Here goes nothing," he tells the image in the mirror. Climbing into his father's overcoat, he tightens the silencer screwed onto the barrel of the .357 Magnum Colt and removes the plastic caps protecting each end of the long, thin cylinder fastened onto the top of the revolver. He flicks on the cylinder's switch. Instantly a needlelike beam of yellow light dances on the wall of the room. Fifteen minutes to five—a good half hour after moonset, according to Roman's Patek Philippe—the Ossetes' new *pakhan* joins the Vladivostok Chamber Orchestra musicians, each armed with a folding-stock PPS-43 fitted with a home-crafted noise suppressor, on the third-floor landing of the fire staircase. Spare thirty-round magazines are taped wrong end up to the magazines inserted in the submachine guns.

Walking single file, the Ossetes start up the stairs. Three enforcers peel off from the group on the fifteenth floor and take up positions facing the fire door in case Caplan's soldiers, wakened by the sound of shooting on the floor above them, unlock the chain and try to use the fire staircase. On the sixteenth-floor landing, Spider slaps small plastic charges onto each of the door's three hinges and a larger charge onto the knob. "Don't blow the door until the lights go out," Roman whispers.

He and Spider study their wristwatches. "Another thirty seconds," Spider mumbles. Roman fits on his night-vision goggles. The Ossetes on the staircase above and below him, taking their cue from the new *pakhan*, pull on their goggles and flip off the safety levers on their PPS-43s. "Ten seconds," Spider announces.

As the second hand on Roman's watch hits the hour, the single light on the landing wall goes dark. Spider yanks the lanyards on his four plastic charges and backs away from the fire door. Seconds later the charges explode, blowing the heavy door off its hinges and onto the carpet in the hallway. Pushing through the smoke, Roman, with the Ossetes on his heels, surges onto the sixteenth floor. One of the armorers, in underpants and holding a shotgun, appears at the door of a room. "What's going—" Snub-nose bullets from two submachine guns hammer into his chest, flinging him back into the room. Other doors farther down the hall fly open as Caplan's brigadiers, shouting to each other in confusion, emerge from their rooms, only to be cut down by short bursts of bullets or by grenades exploding at their feet.

Roman, with Spider and Spare Rib close behind, runs to his right, past the elevator with its door wedged open by a chair. He tries the knob on the last door in the hallway. Finding it locked, he nods to Spider, who slaps a charge onto the knob and pulls hard on the lanyard. The small explosion demolishes the lock and the door swings open on its hinges. Ducking into the suite of rooms, Roman spots Naum Caplan, barefoot and in pajamas, groping along a wall for the light switch. In the greenish hue of the night-vision goggles, Caplan, his hair disheveled, one hand clutching his pajama bottoms to keep them from falling, looks as if he were swimming underwater. He finds the switch and frantically flicks it on and off and on again. When the overhead light fails to work, he stumbles across the room, one arm stretched ahead like a blind man as he feels his way through the darkness to an enormous desk, where he wrenches open a drawer and pulls out a large navy revolver and a box of cartridges. He is jamming bullets into the revolver when he notices the yellow insect dancing on his stomach and tries to brush it away with the back of a hand. The yellow insect vaults up to his chest and then his neck and then his jaw, all the while Caplan slapping at it with his hand until it hits him that he is not dealing with an insect. Squinting, he stares into the pitch-blackness of the room, mesmerized by the long, thin needle of yellow light. When he opens his mouth to scream, the insect leaps into the back of his throat. Across the room there is a muffled blast of air. Caplan, his arms splayed, his pajamas falling to his ankles, is struck by a sledgehammer that hurls him back into the wall. He sinks onto the floor in a sitting position, his head—what is left of it—hanging off to the side at a grotesque angle.

Roman backs out of the room into the hallway, which rings with shouts and curses and the shrill screams of frightened women, and an occasional pistol shot as Caplan's brigadiers, crouching in doorways, fire blindly into the darkness. Roman tries the knob on the door across from Caplan's suite. He is surprised to discover it isn't locked. He'd been vaguely hoping it would be. Pushing it open with his left hand, he steps into the suite and sees Yulia, blinded by the darkness, standing like a statue in the middle of the room. She is wearing a white jumpsuit and fur-lined ankle boots and appears to be underwater in the eerie greenish half-light of the night-vision goggles. "That will surely be you, Roman from another planet," she calls into the darkness. "I knew you would come to murder my father."

"Bloodshed calls out for blood to be shed," Roman murmurs.

"Did he suffer?"

"Half a minute of fear. My father knew he was dying for the better part of a day."

"More spilt milk for Yulia," she groans with a soundless sob. "And have you come to murder me too?"

Roman wades through the sea-green light to grasp one of her wrists. "I have come to take you with me."

"I refuse to go with you."

He slaps her twice, hard, across the face. Through his goggles he sees a torrent of tears spill from her eyes. Tightening his grip on her wrist, he pulls her toward the door and into the hallway. The Ossetes are rolling tear gas grenades down the length of the carpet littered with the dead and the dying. Caplan's brigadiers, coughing and cursing, shout to each other from the rooms. Pitching a few more smoke and tear gas grenades onto the sixteenth floor, the Ossetes pull back to the fire landing as Spider seeds the hallway with packets rigged to explode every two minutes to keep Caplan's surviving brigadiers occupied. Kicking away the chair wedging the elevator doors open, Roman pulls Yulia inside. Spare Rib slips into the elevator behind them as the doors close and Roman stabs at the first subbasement button.

Eight minutes later the night clerk, taking frantic calls from guests on the fourteenth floor claiming to hear gunshots somewhere above them, is astonished to see the Vladivostok Chamber Orchestra musicians, carrying their violin and viola and cello cases, make their way through the lobby to the hotel's double doors and the bus waiting outside with its motor running. "You guys need to settle your minibar bills before you leave," he yells after them. "Oh shit," he mutters. "I am going to catch hell for this."

Lice counts noses when the musicians are safely in the bus. Twelve Ossetes, one of them with his arm in a makeshift sling inside his overcoat, the result of a ricocheting bullet, are accounted for. "Where's the *pakhan*?" Lice shouts. "Anybody seen Roman?"

Spare Rib, the last one to reach the bus, says, "I went down to the garage with him and the girl—"

"What girl?" Lice breathes, his face close to Spare Rib's.

"The girl he brought back from Yalta. He dragged her out of the suite across from Caplan's so I figure she must be his daughter."

"Why would Roman take her to the garage? There was nothing in our plan about the girl or the garage!"

"How the hell would I know?" Spare Rib protests. "Maybe the *pakhan* decided we needed a hostage. She didn't look like she was thrilled to go with him but he sure didn't leave her much choice. He pushed her into a car and drove off with her."

Spider whips the soggy Belomorkanal out of his lips. "Which car, Spare Rib?" he wants to know.

"Which car they drove off in, is that what you are asking me? What difference does it make?"

"Which car, goddamn it!"

"The Porsche, if you must know."

Spider turns white. He grabs hold of a lapel on Lice's overcoat. "We need to stop him," he whispers fiercely.

"How can we stop him when we don't know where—" Suddenly, the kopek drops. "When you rigged the bomb in Caplan's Studebaker that didn't need a new carburetor, you told Timur you rigged a second car. Which car, Spider?"

"We absolutely have got to stop him!" Spider screams.

Yulia leans her cheek against the window of the Porsche, savoring the numbing iciness of the glass. Except for the garbage truck emptying trash cans and a man dressed in a woman's fur coat walking four dogs, Volgogradskiy Prospekt, saturated in buttery yellow from the overhead streetlamps, is deserted. As there are no automobiles in sight on the avenue or the streets that cross it, Roman doesn't bother to stop for the occasional red light. Yulia finally finds her tongue. "Where are we going?" she asks.

"You once told me the climate in Switzerland wasn't cold enough for you. So I'm taking you to Siberia."

Yulia, lost in Timur's cashmere overcoat, offers up a mocking laugh. "As Siberia is several thousand kilometers from here, you will be obliged to stop for gas. When you do I swear I will yell for the police and get you arrested for murdering my father and kidnapping his daughter."

"We won't be stopping for gas. The Siberia I'm taking you to is nearer than you imagine."

"Fuck you, Roman."

"I am definitely fucked," he decides. He is suddenly whelmed by what might have been. "It's on me if we are star-crossed lovers."

Yulia shakes her head. "The goddamn stars have nothing to do with it. There was a moment in Yalta when we could have loosed the knots that bound us to our fathers—we could have scrambled down the sheets tied into strips and escaped the curse of our *vory* families. You threw it away, for fuck's sake! Why, Roman? How could you let this happen? What were you thinking?" She turns to stare at a drunken man lurching from lamppost to hydrant to traffic light as he stumbles along Volgogradskiy Prospekt, but winds up berating her reflection in the car's window. "You should have known this would end badly, Yulia," she tells herself. "Something is seriously wrong with a man who can't deal with yes for an answer." She takes a deep breath. "You're not well, Roman."

"Didn't know they taught psychoanalysis at your Swiss finishing school," he remarks with a mirthless smile.

"You talk crazy. Siberia isn't closer than I imagined. Here's the thing: Love, if you're lucky enough to stumble across it once in a lifetime, is not something you toss away for the fleeting pleasure of revenge." She stares at him in the darkness, catching glimpses of the anguished expression on his face when the Porsche passes under streetlights. "You look crazy too. There is something in your eyes that wasn't there before."

"The something that was in my eyes before this craziness was love for you, Yulia."

"I loved you too," she murmurs. "I am still infected with this love. It was a new experience for me. Now I think of it as a sickness. Now I don't even like you."

He breathes heavily through his nostrils. "You told me like had a longer shelf life than love."

"Not my fault if you turned out to be the exception to the rule." She has a terrifying premonition. "This Siberia of yours will either cure your craziness or kill you."

"I'm already dead, Yulia." He glances quickly at her. "You're dying."

"You're frightening me, Roman." She twists in her seat to gaze at the pinpoints of light filling the night sky.

"The stars you're looking at, they may not exist anymore," he tells her.

"What are you saying? Of course they exist. I can see them still dancing."

"I read somewhere that Arcturus is thirty-eight light-years away. Which means you're seeing an image projected onto your optic nerve by light that left Arcturus when Stalin died."

"What has this—"

"Don't you get it? You won't know if Arcturus existed on Tuesday, January twenty-first, 1992, until 2030."

"Another of your crazy riddles. If Arcturus doesn't exist, someone out there looking down at our planet may decide *we* don't exist. If we don't exist, what's the point of falling in—"

23
POSTSCRIPTUM: BULLETS ARE CHEAPER THAN VASECTOMIES . . .

THE NINTH FLOOR OF THE MVD'S CIRCUMCISED HEADQUARTERS, MOSCOW

Thirteen hours after the raid on the Narodnaya Hotel

Champagne corks are popping in the Sixth Bureau of the Organized Crime Control Department. Osip Axelrod's boss, Alexander Smirnov, pleasantly juiced, brandishes his plastic glass over his bald head. "Nothing quenches thirst like champagne celebrating the death of *vory*!" he exclaims. Draining his glass, he blots his lips on one of the sunflowers printed on his wide silk tie and thrusts out an arm for a refill.

The Sixth Bureau's twenty-six Moscow staffers, most in rumpled civilian suits, several wearing crisp coffee-colored uniforms of frontier guards, along with four female secretaries and the bureau's receptionist in miniskirts, clank their plastic glasses or teacups as they gleefully toast the latest good news in the Great Turf War. Osip Axelrod raps the bayonet he uses to open letters against an empty champagne bottle. "I won't be betraying state secrets," he declares, "if I tell you that the Ossete *vory* killed Naum Caplan, eight of his brigadiers, and an armorer, as well as some poor slob of an accountant who had the misfortune to be on the sixteenth floor of the Narodnaya Hotel."

"Wrong place, wrong time," Axelrod's trainee, Misha, offers with an edgy laugh.

"Six more of Caplan's brigadiers were wounded," Osip adds, "three of them seriously enough to risk winding up in pine coffins. The carnage followed on the heels of the murder of Timur the Lame, the *pakhan* of the Ossete *vory v zakone*, who was something of a legend for living by an antiquated thieves' code of honor. Obviously, the raid on Caplan's *vory* was an act of revenge, a settling of scores."

"If we know the attackers were Ossetes, what's stopping us from arresting them for murder?" demands Boris Ivanov, who, before being posted to the ninth floor of the circumcised MVD headquarters the previous week, ran the Sixth Bureau's operation at Sheremetyevo International Airport.

Alexander Smirnov helps himself to one of the zakuski warmed in the office microwave by the secretaries. "There is good news and there is bad news," he announces, talking with his mouth full. "The good news," he asserts cheerfully, "is it's hard to imagine what's left of Caplan's Jew *vory* recovering from this *razborka*."

Several staffers stare at their shoes in embarrassment. Osip Axelrod steps up to fill the awkward silence. "The director is not suggesting we are celebrating Caplan's demise because he was an Israelite. We celebrate it because he was a gangster bleeding honest businessmen white when he wasn't murdering Ossetes."

"Ex-sactly," Alexander Smirnov, slurring the word, agrees.

"You said something about bad news," Axelrod reminds his boss.

"How about skipping the bad news for once?" the

receptionist suggests, drawing a smattering of half-hearted applause from the Moscow staffers.

But Alexander Smirnov is not to be put off. "The news that is bad . . . The bad news is, there is no way—no goddamn way—to pin murder charges on the Ossetes."

The director, seldom at a loss for words, appears to run out of things to say. Axelrod elaborates on the director's bad news. "The two hotel employees who actually came face to face with the self-styled impresario—the desk clerk when the bogus Vladivostok Chamber Orchestra checked in, the night porter who brought the Samsonite filled with grenades to his room—swear the fellow was a Uighur. Both are too terrified of *vory v zakone* to testify against one in open court."

"What about fingerprints?" Boris Ivanov asks.

Osip Axelrod concentrates on his teacup. "If you had taken the time to read the action postmortem," he lectures Ivanov, whom he disliked at first sight when he reported for duty in Moscow wearing a Communist Party pin in his lapel, "you would discover that the so-called musicians all wore gloves—all the time." Axelrod polishes off what's left of the champagne in his teacup. "As for the Ossetes," he plunges on as Misha provides him with a refill, "I can say that after the poisoning of their *pakhan*, the *vor* Timur the Lame, we took it for granted his son, Roman, would step into his shoes. In our line of work, they school us to expect the unexpected, but I have to admit what happened next was off the page. We think the new *pakhan*, Roman Timurovich, along with Caplan's daughter, Yulia Naumovna, may have been in the Porsche that exploded on Volgogradskiy Prospekt early this morning. The police collected a sackful of body parts. We're still waiting on a definitive ID from their forensic people."

Boris Ivanov, smarting from Axelrod's very public rebuke

and hoping to have the last word, sneers, "Good riddance to rotten rubbish! I personally interviewed this Roman Timurovich at the airport when he came back from England. I can say he was an arrogant son of a bitch. He expected us to reimburse him for the shaving cream we spilled searching his duffel. If it had been up to me, I would have put him on the first plane back to England, but their MI5 people don't take kindly to our returning merchandise they went to the trouble of shipping us."

Director Smirnov, who is not comfortable with dissension in the ranks, tries to change the subject. "Assuming forensics confirms the identity of the deceased," he puts the question to the chief of his department's Sixth Bureau, "do we have a clue, an inkling, a sneaking suspicion, a theory even, that could explain what the Jewess and the Ossete were doing together in the Porsche?" Smirnov laughs a bit wildly. "Talk about strange bedfellows!"

"That is something of a mystery," Axelrod admits. "You would have thought, given what happened to their fathers, they would have cut each other's throat if they got half a chance. There's another mystery, Chief—the Porsche was heading east when it blew up. If one or both of these individuals were fleeing the scene of a crime, you would expect them to head west, toward Berlin now that there is no wall, by way of Poland."

"Maybe they were on their way to Japan by way of Siberia," the secretary passing around zakuski jokes with a giggle.

"Nobody puts a foot in Siberia if they can help it," another secretary remarks.

"Who knows where they were going," Alexander Smirnov growls. "In the end, who gives a flying f . . ." He remembers there are females in the room. ". . . who gives a damn. The bottom line . . . The line at the bottom . . ." He puts a hand on a desk to steady himself. "I lost my thought."

"You were identifying the bottom line?" Axelrod prompts him.

"Yes, yes, surely the bottom line is, thanks to the diligent work of our Organized Crime Control team, and most particularly Osip Axelrod's Sixth Bureau, the thieves' world is less populated today."

"We may have stumbled on a new form of population control," the receptionist declares with a suggestive smirk.

"Bullets are cheaper than vasectomies," an older staffer quips.

"To thieves' funerals," Smirnov blurts out, hiking his glass in a toast. "The only good *vor* is a dead *vor*."

Boris Ivanov, eager to massage the ego of the chief, raises his teacup to salute the Organized Crime Control director. "*Uraa*, esteemed Alexander Smirnov!"

The others, knowing what is expected of them, pick up the mantra in embarrassed chorus, repeating it three times for the Holy Trinity. "*Uraa! Uraaa! Uraaaa!*"

Only Osip Axelrod, lost in discomfiting hindsight—was Timur the Lame's fossilized thieves' code a scourge of the seventy-year Soviet plague or its saving grace?—neglects to join the feeble chorus. The deafening silence of Mother Russia's collective conscience, and his own complicity in *bullets are cheaper than vasectomies*, scalds his eardrums.